ULYSSES GRANT:

Youth to Uniform

A Historical Novel by

Joe Krom

EEL RIVER
TRADERS

ULYSSES GRANT: Youth to Uniform
by Joe Krom

© 2014 Joseph A Krom

Permissions: info@eelrivertraders.com

ISBN 978-0-692-40603-8

Library of Congress control number 2015904822

Printed in USA
Edition 1 – 2015

Published by Eel River Traders
10610 18th Rd., Argos, IN 46501
www.eelrivertraders.com

PREFACE

Gen. R.A. Alger
Address at Grant's Tomb
Memorial Day 1890

General Grant was not an ideal soldier in appearance. He had none of the dash and fire such as artists paint and poets glorify, but he had within a calm, determined purpose to meet whatever duties fell to his lot, and to discharge them to the best of his ability.

It is a law of nature that in animal, as well as vegetable life, that which grows rapidly and matures early lasts but little time. The firmest fibers of wood are those of steady but slow growth. The fruit that lasts longest and holds its flavor best is long in maturing. So with men.

C ..... Cincinnati	Nz .... Natchez
G ..... Galena	Ph .... Philadelphia
H ..... Harrisburg	Pt .... Pittsburgh
J ..... Fort Jesup	S ..... St. Louis
L ..... Louisville	T ..... Fort Towson
Mr ... Marietta	Wh ... Wheeling
My ... Maysville	WP ... West Point
NO .. New Orleans	

INDIANA

OHIO

Cincinnati

Bethel

New Richmond

Pt. Pleasant

Georgetown

Higginsport

Ripley

Augusta

KENTUCKY

Maysville

ACKNOWLEDGEMENTS

My wife Anita assisted with this book in innumerable ways. She traveled with me north, south, east, and west while visiting sites, museums, and libraries. She took hundreds of notes. She read my manuscript time and again. She has been a continual source of encouragement.

I am indebted to my readers for their insights and comments: Daniel Voreis; John Haste, MD; and Capt. Richard W. Krom, USN (Ret).

I thank the staffs of the following institutions for sharing their resources:
Brown County Public Library, Georgetown, OH
Brown County Recorder's Office, Georgetown, OH
Cincinnati History Museum, Cincinnati, OH
Fort Jesup State Historic Site, Many, LA
Galena & U.S. Grant Museum, Galena, IL
Galina Public Library, Galina, IL
Harriet Beecher Stowe House, Cincinnati, OH
Hesburgh Library, Univ. of Notre Dame, South Bend, IN
Kentucky Gateway Museum Center, Maysville, KY
National Underground Railroad Freedom Center, Cincinnati, OH
Rankin House, Ripley, OH
Slavery to Freedom Museum – Historic Washington, Washington, KY
Ulysses S. Grant National Historic Site, St. Louis, MO
Ulysses S. Grant Presidential Library –
                    Mississippi State Univ., Starkville, MS
U.S. Grant Boyhood Home and Schoolhouse, Georgetown, OH
West Point Museum, USMA, West Point, NY

CONTENTS

White Oak Creek

The orange glow of the setting sun did not linger in the narrow gorge of White Oak Creek. Twilight quickly gave way to dusk, and dusk to a deep lingering darkness. On a platform of limestone near tumbling waters a fire dimly lit a circle in the blackness of the ravine. More than a camp fire, less than a bonfire, its flicker glowed against a canopy of overhanging leaves. Shadows bounced upon a scarred cliff face. A pervasive silence enveloped the forest, tempered by the murmur of cascading water and an occasional pop from a fire log.

The creek bounded its way southward through a crooked descent to join the Ohio River some eight miles distant. Its bed consisted of a jumble of boulders, rapids upon rapids its course. Occasionally a distinct, though small, waterfall churned the flow to foam. Much of the year the current was but a mere trickle between small pools. Spring rains had now swollen it to a surging river.

A boy of twelve years and one week stood wrapped in a blanket, his back to the fire. Beside him clothes hung from stretched limbs. A pair of boots was held upside down by two stakes a safe distance from the heat. Close by a shelter was formed by a canvas tied to trees in its front and to wooden spokes of a grain wagon in the back. Horse collars and heavy harness hung from the front of the wagon. Fishing poles leaning against a fallen tree trunk revealed the purpose of the little camp.

Young Ulysses checked first his clothes, then his boots. He flapped his blanket and slowly turned a circle to warm himself. A second boy, three years older, stacked tin plates and headed for the stream. Beyond the fire, two younger rambunctious boys jostled and giggled.

Dan informed his friend, "I'll clean up, then I'll look after the horses."

Lyss replied, "You'll likely spook the horses. I will look in on them just as soon as I stop shivering."

Dan, "Yah, and the sun will be up before then. You may be the champion horseman of all the boys in the county, but I can at least tend to a team of staked horses."

Lyss, "My clothes will be dry enough by the time you get back. I'll do it." He called to the younger boys, "You boys settle down! Look around and see that no food is left lay. We don't want any bears rummaging through camp tonight."

Sim, "Ain't no bears here. You can't scare me. Hain't been nary a bear, nor buffalo, nor wolf around here for twenty years. Old man Upham told me so, and Pa agreed."

Lyss, "May be so, but there are coons and skunks. You want a skunk in your bed?"

The younger boys went on tussling. Lyss grabbed his shirt and began dressing.

Johnny, "I'm still hungry!"

Lyss, "You had three fish and two potatoes – and some of my bread."

Johnny called to his older cousin, "But I'm still hungry. Where are the sausages that you brought?"

Lyss replied, "Those are for breakfast. You can just forget about any more cooking tonight."

Sim tagged Johnny. "You're it!" Off he ran into the brush. Johnny dove after him.

Lyss pulled on his boots, fastened his suspenders, and headed down a narrow path to a patch of grass where he had staked the horses. Dan returned from his chore. He used a pole to rearrange the fire logs. The flame grew higher; the arc of light grew brighter. He climbed into the wagon and located his sack of supplies. Cornbread muffins and apple butter were in order for everyone after an active day. He set out the little feast and puttered about the camp. Lyss returned and pitched more wood on the fire.

Dan inquired, "You still cold? The fire is already too big."

Lyss, "There's plenty of wood on the stack. Besides, I heard something out there along the path. Don't know exactly what it was."

Dan, "What do you think it was? What did it sound like?"

Lyss, "I don't know, just weird." He squinted into the darkness, "But no matter, probably nothing."

The two young friends munched their snack and let their thoughts drift to fishing and rock climbing and freedom from chores of home. They heard their younger companions romping and laughing. They contemplated ghost stories they could tell when the fire grew old, when they had all snuggled into their makeshift beds.

Dan shared, "Lyss, thanks for arranging the wagon and everything. I don't get out of town much the way you do. Here I am the elder, but you've seen more country and villages and towns than I have. There aren't many boys your age that their father would let take a team and wagon as far off by themselves as you are accustomed to. Sure it's still work, but it is more adventurous than every day in a print shop. People seem to think a newspaper is exciting, but for a boy my age there is little excitement in ink and typesetting. People stop by to tell their story. We get all the gossip and hear about all the events. But hearing is not being a part of it. I only get to reflect upon other people's adventures."

Lyss, "It's only natural that a man expects his eldest son to take up his trade and some day perpetuate it. You're helping your dad in his business. At the same instant he's teaching you his trade." Once again he fueled the fire. "I know that I will always be a disappointment to my Pa. I'll never be a tanner, and he knows it. I just can't ever step into that tannery without thinking about the poor animals who wore those skins – skins that are being dipped and soaked and scraped. I try to not think about it, but I get sick to my stomach every time. I'll never make a tanner. So, Pa sends me out on whatever errand comes up. I'm good with horses and that helps out."

Dan, "Yeah, I've heard your Pa tell my Dad about it. He cannot comprehend your aversion to the tannery. But, he is proud of your knack with horses. 'Uncanny' he calls it. Of course, him being in the print shop more than anyone else, I hear him talk."

Lyss, "Yes, you hear him talk. The whole town, if not the whole county, make that the entire state, hears him talk. His letters to the editor aren't enough – he has your Dad print up tracts and pamphlets that he passes out to everyone. I just wish he would be satisfied running a business."

Dan, "Townsfolk do get irritated with him. He has an argumentative disposition. But he does seem to be a good businessman. He's been mayor of Georgetown, hasn't he, and president of the lodge?" They sat quietly for a brief stint. "I never thought about one day taking over the newspaper. No, I don't think that's for me. I see myself one day as captain of a tall-masted ship on the open seas. If not, maybe a steamboat bound for New Orleans."

The younger boys came running in, wide-eyed and breathless.

Johnny, "We, we, we saw!"

Sim, "We saw someone in the woods! They ran away, that way, upstream!"

Johnny, "Maybe there were two of them!"

Dan, "Calm down. Are you sure it wasn't a deer? Maybe a dog or fox?"

Johnny, "I think it was a man. It was dark. He started running."

Sim, "I think it could have been a woman. It was too dark to tell."

Dan grabbed a stout stick and peered into the darkness around the perimeter of the camp. Lyss stepped to the wagon's tool box and pulled out a pistol. He quickly checked it over, then hid it in his blankets. He instructed his brother Sim to fuel the fire.

Lyss, "You boys aren't pulling a prank, are you?"

Boys, "No, sir!" "No, sir!"

Dan spoke half convincingly, "Well, if someone was out there, they've skedaddled. Here, have some muffins. Warm up by the flame. Don't go romping around anymore."

Lyss, "A dark night in the woods can play tricks on the eyes."

To distract the boys, and perhaps himself, Lyss began reminding Dan about shared events that entered his mind: snowball fights; the broken window in the courthouse; the largest fish.

Dan stomped out a spark that had found dry weeds. He had gone only four steps when a lantern was thrust into his face. A gruff hand grabbed his shoulder and stopped him in his tracks.

Voice in the dark, "Whar ya think yer goin' boy? Git back thar with them others!"

Dan was shoved back. Lyss jumped up. Suddenly there were three lanterns and three voices.

"How many ya got in thar?" "Who are ye?" "Look in

the wagon!" "Why, they're jist boys!"

First voice, "Wots your name, boy?"

Dan lied, "Levi Mount." He gave the name of the bully from the far side of Georgetown.

"And you?" the voice asked Lyss.

"Hiram Ulysses, sir." Not lying, but still misleading, he took a tip from Dan. He used his first and middle name, omitting "Grant", his family name. "That's my brother Simpson. Leave him be. He's just a lad. And my cousin Johnny Marshall."

Dan tried to sound resolute. "What's this about? We've done no harm!" He had a great suspicion of what it was about.

Voice, "You boys step out here so I can look at ye! Jud, look around and see what you cin find. Hank, check thet wagon. Now, what you young folks doin' out here in this gully? Any cabins here abouts?"

What had been a bulky shadow sashayed up and took on the form of a tough scalawag.

Dan mustered his courage as best he could and took charge, "Just a little fishing excursion. Just the four of us out of Georgetown. We come here regular, when we can. The fishing's good just below a little waterfall there. We did alright, but the water's high, making it a little difficult."

"Whar's yer fish?"

"Ate 'em. There's our sapling poles and bait. We plan on fishing 'till noon tomorrow, then head back – folks will be expecting us."

The two roughnecks motioned to the leader that

nothing of significance was found. "Just some vittles."

The intruders backed off, but kept their eyes focused on the flabbergasted campers. Each man sat and laid an old long shotgun across his lap. They hitched their knife sheaths around to a ready position. Lyss took a half step back and put his foot on the blanket that was covering his pistol.

The leader gave a sinister smile and softened his voice, "'Pologize for startling you young'uns. We're huntin' quail and one of our party got hisself lost. We's jist out lookin' fer 'im. Thought he might 'uv come this away. You seen anybody?"

Dan responded, "We just had supper and cleaned up. It's dark down here. If anyone came this way, it's not likely we would see him unless he stepped into the light. I hope he finds his way back. It's mighty dangerous out here with the high water and the slippery rocks and all. My friend here already fell in once. The walls of this ravine close right in against the creek in places. You can't cross the creek right now, especially in the dark. The terrain is not the only obstacle. There's a band of men who call themselves the Squirrel Hunters Club. They got that name because every man can down a squirrel at fifty yards and not have to shoot twice. Stories are that they go out at night and harass slave hunters that come up across the Ohio River. They see it as an insult to Brown County that bounty hunters have to chase slaves into our state of Ohio when they can't catch them in Kentucky. Us young boys don't know who's in the Squirrel Hunters, but stories abound about slave chasers disappearing,

[8]

never to be seen again. They would just as soon shoot a slave chaser as hang a horse thief. No, sir, I wouldn't want to tangle with them on a dark night. I sure wouldn't want you gentlemen to be mistaken for bounty hunters. Then there's prowling panthers!"

The leader cut him off, "We have panthers, too. And we're no slave hunters – quail hunters, that's all there's to it. Why are you talkin' so funny. You're a Yankee boy if'n I ever seen one."

Dan, "Well, that's a good thing that you're just hunting. For those old fowling pieces would be no match for the Squirrel Hunter guns, no, sir. Good luck with your birding. Hope you find your lost fellow. If he shows up here we'll be sure to tell him you are out looking. Sorry we don't have any fish left to send with you."

The three visitors slowly got up and tromped off whence they came.

Dan directed the boys back into their blankets, "Stay quiet."

There was no protest. The two younger boys dove in and covered their heads. Dan and Lyss knelt and listened intently.

Eventually Lyss asked, "What do you think? Quail hunters?"

Dan, "You are so naive. Just because you never lie doesn't mean others won't. Everything about that crew says rapscallions from well beyond the Ohio River. Besides, why would anyone not from these parts come up here to hunt quail? Ever since you heard that noise earlier and the boys saw someone fleeing through the trees, I have been thinking 'runaways.' And where there are runaway slaves you can count on slave chasers close behind. We're just lucky the runaways didn't stop here for warmth and food, for surely we would have provided it. Now we would be standing at the wrong end of those old guns. Or you would have gone for your pistol to defend us and we would all be shot graveyard dead."

Lyss, "You know, I would have defended us and, yes, defended the runaways, too. Imagine being chased night and day, mile upon mile, meeting obstacle upon obstacle, afraid to stop, afraid to sleep. Who could you trust? Where could you find shelter? When and where would you eat next? Here we sat with our canvas and blankets, with our fire, eating muffins, bellies full of fish. We could have tossed muffins into the brush. I would have given my pistol. What runaways that may have been out there are gone now. It must be terrible."

Dan, "Don't you know, there are those who guide the runaways, leading them from place to place until they reach safety? Sometimes they go on their own. Often, those who have made it to Canada can't resist returning south for wives, husbands, children, mothers, or lovers. I've heard talk of them franticly beating on doors in the middle of the night begging for mercy, a morsel to eat, which direction to go, sometimes to be taken in. The wrong door could mean being captured and turned over to the Sheriff Clarence. Old Clarence has no choice, he's sworn to uphold the law."

Lyss, "Well, this night's runaways don't have much of a start. The chasers are hot on their trail."

Dan, "If the malefactors had hounds, they would have snared their prize for sure. I suspect there are dogs. Maybe the sharp rocks cut the dogs' feet and they had to turn back."

Lyss' face grew stern, "I'm going out to find the runaways and help them along!"

Dan, "You are not! Likely you would lead those foul men directly to their quarry. They are probably still watching us. They can't do much more than flounder around this rocky ravine tonight, that is, unless you head out and show them the way."

Lyss, "I just wish I could be of some help to those poor souls in their quest for freedom. Lord, have mercy upon them!" After reflection, "Do you think there are people in Georgetown who take them in, who guide them along their way?"

Dan lowered his voice, "I don't know, but I've wondered. You know that at least half of Georgetown is of southern disposition. But those of the Yankee persuasion are resolute. Think about it. Who are the most outspoken abolitionists in town?"

Lyss thought out loud, "Well, our Methodist preacher, I suppose."

Dan, "Right! Ever since Reverend Maley came to town people have been swarming to the Methodist Church."

Lyss, "Then there's Thomas Morris over at Bethel."

Dan, "Yes, but think now, who talks the most publicly against slavery?"

Lyss, "I guess Pa and your Dad."

Dan, "Right. Who is to say that they not only proclaim abolitionist doctrine, but assist runaways as well?"

Lyss, "Well, all I know is there are none in our root cellar."

Dan, "I just wonder if they couldn't be organizers, ones who set up the routes and places of safety. Not alone, but in cahoots with leaders in other towns. I don't know, but I have been wondering."

Lyss, "I just can't picture Pa like that. I just can't."

Dan, "Think about it. How many times have you driven your Pa to slavery debates where he took part in the addresses? You took him more than once to the fiery debates at that Lane Seminary in Cincinnati. You said that you even sat in Lyman Beecher's parlor one afternoon."

Lyss, "Yeah, the finest house I've ever been in – a mansion on a hill. Crazy thing is, his daughters are teachers. Have you ever heard the like? Can you image having a lady teacher? Reverend Beecher introduced us; I just cringed like a scolded child."

Dan, "You can't get any more abolitionist than Beecher!"

Lyss, "I just drove the buggy and waited around during the meetings. All the talk sounded the same to me."

Dan, "You saw that I didn't use my real name tonight. Maybe those chasers have been in the region long enough to have heard about a newspaperman named Ammen who publishes for the abolitionists. I didn't want to take a chance on them making a connection. Dad told me that some years back an abolitionist newspaper in Cincinnati was smashed up and the editor run out of town. He says that he uses caution in what he prints and what he does not. Says that if he hires a freeman the rabble will come after him for sure."

Lyss, "Pa hires freemen."

Dan, "Yes, but not in the tannery, not in town. He only uses them in the woods cutting timber and chopping bark for tanning."

Lyss, "You forget, our house servant is a freeman."

Dan, "As long as he is a servant, they don't mind."

Lyss, "You certainly have contemplated this more than I have."

Dan, "When we get back, let's each tell our fathers about tonight and watch their reactions. If they are overly inquisitive it will be an indication."

Ulysses' mind ran through events for hints that may substantiate Dan's affirmations. Had not his father often told him that he had left Maysville, Kentucky to leave slavery behind? He had apprenticed there at Uncle Peter Grant's tannery for five years, "more than long enough to witness the evils of slavery." His father had told him about the year working in the tannery of Owen Brown up in Hudson, Ohio. Owen had taken his new journeyman apprentice to hear all of the anti-slavery speakers that passed through. Owen's boy, John, would quote scripture proving the sinfulness of slavery. Pa would always comment, "Whenever John Brown got to commenting on slavery and scripture, he would just fly off the handle. He'd talk for an hour whether anyone was listening or not, totally useless for work until the next day." Ulysses thought about the frequent anti-slavery sermons he had heard at the Methodist Church just across the street from his home. Were members there active on behalf of fleeing slaves? He had never really paid that much attention. He half convinced himself that his mother's parents, the Simpsons living west of Bethel, were guiding slaves to freedom. One indication after another fell into place. But, surely not, it was too much to grasp. He pushed it out of his mind.

Lyss, "Dan, thanks for pulling me out of the drink today."

Dan, "If it hadn't been for that overhanging tree, I wouldn't have been able to reach you. You should thank God for that tree."

Lyss, "I have already thanked him for your presence and your strength."

Dan, "Imagine, me saving you, you being the better swimmer. How did you get swept into the stream?"

Lyss, "All I remember is that I took a few steps out on a poplar log. I slipped. I saw stars and everything went blank until you pulled me up on the bank."

Dan, "Lyss."

Lyss, "Yes?"

Dan, "Thank you for not trying to shoot those intruders."

Georgetown Woods

Steel rims on wooden wheels bumped and rattled along the hard packed country road. Tufts of dust followed in their wake. Spring rains had long been forsaken by summer doldrums. Spring ruts were now turned to rock-hard furrows. Passing young corn stalks and tobacco plants baking under the unyielding summer sun, the wagon kept a steady pace. The slow-turning wooden spoke wheels jostled from groove to groove.

Young Hiram Ulysses Grant, now thirteen, leaned forward in the spring seat. He spread wide his feet and hunched his body. He had long ago learned how to limber his muscles and sway with the wagon to minimize jolts. He let the team of horses set their own pace through the growing heat. The massive beasts knew their work. They knew the road. They knew the firm, yet gentle, temperament of the teamster. They could not know that this day would end early due to Independence Day celebrations.

Lyss spoke placid encouragement to his team, "Doin'

fine there, Jake. Atta way, Molly. Keep a steppin'."

This was his second trip today to the hundred-acre woods. His father had purchased the forested land a mile northeast of Georgetown from Senator Thomas Morris. The land served to provide essential bark for the tanning process. Timber from debarked oak trees was being harvested into beams. The beams would repay the cost of the land, and the cleared land would eventually be resold at a profit as farm ground. Limbs too small for milling would fire tanning vats, the excess sold in town for firewood.

His first trip during the cool of the day, if it could be called "cool," brought in a load of sawyer logs. He had tended to the horses while the tannery yard workers unloaded. He then installed sideboards on the wagon – three boards high. With a quick stop at the house he picked up his lunch. His mother sent him to the cellar to get a half sack of potatoes and a half sack of onions to take to the timber cutters. To this she added a freshly baked cherry pie. He ran to the stable to fetch a bundle of straw to nest the vegetables during the bruising ride. Once again he headed up the hill and out of town. The object was a load of tan bark.

July 4, 1835, brought anticipation of holiday feast and frolic. Political orators would pontificate from the podium on the public square. The five Revolutionary War soldiers would be given a rousing ovation. Veterans of the Indian Wars would get their turn followed by 1812 officers and soldiers. Of course Jesse Grant, though no veteran, would find an opportunity to take the platform.

The whole town would then tromp to a field at the north end for horse racing and shooting contests. Lyss planned to apply his skill to pistol shooting competition where likely as not he should make the final round. All this would be followed by artillery and rocket fire. But all festivities would have to wait until later in the evening, after the day's work was complete.

When he had passed the King's place on an earlier trip out and back, he had noticed Lucy King watching him from behind the pump beyond the house. The Kings had substantial farm buildings and quality stock. The two-story brick house testified to a prosperous farm. Lucy, a year junior to Lyss, attended the Dutch Hill subscription school during the winter, the same as Lyss. She was among the group of girls who had packed into his sleigh on snowy days for rides through the countryside. At the head of a long straight downhill stretch he would tease, "Let's make the dashboard earn its title!" The girls would squeal with glee. Frolic had been the order of the day! His thanks? They teased him about having a "pretty doll face" due to his pink skin and rosy cheeks. Now on this trip back to the woods here she was, standing ahead along the roadside outside their gate. She was wearing her Sunday dress with curled hair and a bow. He chose to ignore her. Girls didn't make him nervous, just girls in petticoats and curls.

"Lyss, stop! Stop that wagon!" Lucy called. "I want to talk to you!"

Lyss snapped the reins, "Can't. Work to do."

Lucy, "You just stop! Please stop for a moment. I

[17]

have some cool milk from the springhouse ready. And there's fresh raspberries I picked in this morning's dew." She began trotting alongside, "If you come up to the porch, I'll let you kiss me!"

A slight tug on the reins stopped the wagon. "Now, why are you being such a silly girl? You can see that I have responsibilities. People depend on me."

Lucy, "You're no fun! You and your responsibilities! You and your horses! You never take time to be just a boy."

Lyss, "I do plenty of fishing and exploring. I sled and skate. What about those sleigh rides?"

Lucy, "Yes, but I want to talk to you alone. Just you and me. Please!"

Lyss was growing warm, first in his gut, then in his head. His throat tightened. He wasn't sure why. He just knew that it wasn't all due to the summer sun. He asked, "Don't you have chores? Why has your mother let you dress so early for the picnics? That dress is too nice, anyway."

Lucy, "My parents aren't here. They left two days ago for the Wabash country up in Indiana. They plan to speculate on some Pottawatomie land that is opening up. They'll be gone up to three weeks. Logansport, I think, is their destination."

Lyss, "So, it's just you and Billy. You should have double the chores. That dress won't do for that."

Lucy, "Billy left this morning after feeding the stock. He's gone to Williamsburg. Gone courting he has. Says he won't be back for two days. My guess is he will be at least three. Please come down. I don't like being alone."

Lyss, "I will stop on the way back after I get my load. I can take you to your Aunt Betsy's in town. That's where you should be. You shouldn't be out here alone."

Lucy, "I can't leave the place unattended. Besides, that would give up Billy to Aunt Betsy. Sure, he's wrong to take off like that. But that doesn't mean that I'll give him up."

Lyss, "Alright, listen. I will stop on my way back to town and have that cup of milk – out here by the gate, not on the porch. And you be in your riding clothes, no dress. You can tie your colt to the wagon and ride up here in the seat to town. You can visit with Ma whilst I finish up. Then this evening you can tag along and later we'll ride back here and I will see you are safe inside. Deal?"

Lucy, "My riding colt isn't thoroughly broken."

Lyss, "I will ride your colt and you can ride mine."

"The one you bought for twenty-five dollars from Mr. Ralston?" Lucy laughed.

Ulysses soured at the barb. The whole county knew the story about his buying the colt. It was his first purchase. He had told his father that he knew of the uncommonly fine colt that was for sale and he wanted to purchase it for twenty-five dollars. His father had permitted him to go ahead, only to first offer twenty dollars. If the initial offer was not accepted he should offer twenty-two fifty, and if that was not accepted to offer a final stand at twenty-five. Upon meeting Mr. Ralston, he told him that he was interested in the colt.

"What's your offer?" Mr. Ralston grinned.

"Well," informed Lyss "my father says to open with twenty even, and if that doesn't do it then twenty-two fifty, and if you refuse that then stand firm at twenty-five."

Lyss took the colt home that day for twenty-five dollars. The tale became folklore across Georgetown. He always felt justified in his defense that he was only eight at the time. Also the horse proved four years of good service. Lyss recently sold him for the same twenty-five dollars when it went blind. His defense didn't seem to carry much weight with the other boys of Georgetown.

Ulysses thought about Lucy's young colt. He hesitated for a moment, "This isn't a trick to get me to break your colt, is it? Dr. Brown once tricked me into breaking a carriage horse to pace for the price of delivering a package. Excuse me, but I've learned to shy back when it comes to horse deals, buying, trading, or training."

A tear glistened in Lucinda's eye, "Do you think that I am here to be mean to you?" She turned her head. Her stance slumped.

Lyss, "I'll be back. It will be a couple hours, maybe a little longer. I'll eat lunch with the woodchoppers. You be ready!"

Lucy, "You could have your lunch here, under the shade tree."

Lyss, "I'll be back. You step back now." He gave the reins a quick snap.

Lucy called out, "I'll be here! I'll be ready! I'm

making sweet rolls!" She stepped into the middle of the dirt road watching until he disappeared over the crest.

Ulysses continued on his way, his head spinning. What was it all about? What had he promised? He had planned some wonderful pranks for the celebration. Now Lucy was going to mess everything up. He couldn't avoid returning past the King place. And that frilly dress! The sun beat down. His mind dulled. Time seemed to collapse.

He was still trying to figure everything out when the horses automatically turned onto the lane leading to the back section of woods. The smell of burning brush grew heavy as his wagon left the road behind. The sound of axes whacking into trees resounded as he neared the camp. Jake and Molly drew up near stacked timber.

Ulysses grew to his senses, "Not here, move on!" He guided them ahead to the bark pile. He maneuvered close to the mound while catching as much shade as possible for the team. "Whoa now, steady."

He grabbed his lunch tin, milk tin, and the pie. He made a second trip for the two burlap sacks. He went over to a log under a crooked walnut tree, a place where often he took his lunch. He hung his hat on a low hanging limb. Straddling the log, he laid out his meager meal. Even with the shade the still air parched his throat. He mentally calculated how long to rest the horses against the growing heat for the return trip.

From behind a burning brush heap came Hannibal, foreman of the choppers. His narrow shoulders and lean frame belied his hard-won strength. The tune he whistled revealed a man at peace with himself and his maker. He was followed by two other black men, taller, shirtless, muscles bulging. The two went to the waiting bark and grabbed pitchforks. Hannibal came ahead carrying a bandanna bundle and a jug. Another man, unknown to Ulysses, a new hand, drove a team dragging a pair of logs out of the trees to the timber stack.

"Ahoy, Young Master Grant!" Hannibal called. "Welcome back to Break Neck Woods! Ha! That's what the boys and me call the place now. Makes the place seem more like home if it has a name, don't cha' think?" He took a seat facing Ulysses. His bandanna became his tablecloth. "We finished us a second lean-to last night after work to make room for the new men. I tell you, them boys is good workers. Yes, sir, no doubt about it."

Ulysses liked to listen to Hannibal's slow rhythmic style of talk. Hannibal lived somewhat over ten miles north at one of the Gist Settlements. The whole settlement lot, men, women, and children, some three hundred strong, had been relocated there from Virginia. The plantation owner Gist had specified in his will that all his slaves were to be given their freedom upon his death. His heirs honored his wish and arranged for land and transportation for the relocation. The group became freeman pioneers, working the land and hiring out their skills when they could.

Lyss objected to the title attributed to him, "Call me Lyss, everyone does. I've asked you before, please remember. Or Ulysses"

Hannibal replied, "Sorry, no offense. It's custom

where I come from. Listen to what I have to say so you can tell Master Grant. The new hires will work out fine. We will have the back twenty acres cleared and cleaned out by fall. Some of the largest logs will have to wait for frozen ground and snow to be drug out. Got that?"

Lyss, "Sure, twenty acres ready to sell by fall. Maybe I should take time to see what's been cleared and look over your camp in case Pa has questions. I should meet the new men."

Hannibal's face grew stern, an uncommon occurrence for him, "Now slow down, young man. You do not want to meet those men and you do not want to see too much. It's fine for you to journey here to the staging lot, but don't be going farther back. Master Grant's orders. He will come himself if he needs an inspection. He's welcome any day, yes sir."

Ulysses picked up the vegetable sacks from the back side of the log and set them down on the near side, "Ma sent some vittles."

Hannibal, "Well bless her soul! If she ain't the kindest woman in all the land. She surely has been good to me."

Lyss brought forth the pie, "And a special treat."

Hannibal, "My, oh my! Now how can I get this back to camp without the others seeing it? I'll bring it out for our celebration tonight."

Ulysses replaced the lid on his lunch tin and wiped his hands on his pant legs.

Hannibal took him by the arm. "Indulge me a moment, Young Ulysses. I have a plan I've been thinking on. I'd like to share it with you, kind of a trial run-through." Hannibal folded his bandanna and placed it in his pocket. "It's like this. Times are lean on the settlement – a dearth of prospects, you could say. I'm thinkin' of striking out on my own – a place for my family. If Master Grant would set aside five acres for me to have as my own, I would use two acres of the timber to build me a cabin and shed. I spied a good stand of poplar back yonder. Three acres I would clear myself and give him back the timber. I would stump out the twenty acres we clear this summer and another twenty acres next year. Master Grant would need to supply oxen and their feed. Forty acres of stumpin' in exchange for five acres of land. With five acres and a cabin, my family could have a couple of cows, some hogs and chickens, room for vegetables and crops. I would be here year 'round to keep an eye on things – a permanent caretaker of the woods.

"When the hundred acres of trees are gone and cuttin' runs out, I would be close enough to Georgetown to find work there. I'm a fair carpenter, I'll have ya know. Right now my tools are a bit on the shoddy side. If I can get settled down here close to a growing town, I hope to work my way up to a full set of bona-fide tools. Once I show what I can do and make my mark with some townsfolk, I expect to see steady customers. That's my idea.

"What I'm after is a chance to provide for my wife and boy more than just a place out of the wind and some grub to eat. You should meet Jenny someday. She can sing sweeter than any bluebird you ever heard. She does magic with a piece of cloth and a needle. She takes in sewing work when she can find it. She works mighty hard at making our shack a home, but she deserves better. A good God-fearing woman she is – good and true as the day is long.

"Not that I don't 'preciate this job that Master Grant is providin'. It's a step up, for sure! Bein' out here away from the settlement, well, it gives me a clear way of seein' things. It gives me time to think in a new way."

Lyss took it all in and replied, "Sounds to me like a fair deal and a good plan. But you will have to lay it out for Pa yourself. I have no influence with him. If I said anything, it would likely hurt your cause."

Hannibal, "Not him, your Ma! If you could just slightly mention it to Mistress Grant, I would be much obliged. Later I will go directly to Master Grant with it."

Lyss, "Ma has no influence, neither, not on business matters."

Hannibal, "Young Ulysses, you have things to learn about how families operate. Give it a try and let's see, if you would."

Ulysses knew that his mother took to heart everything she heard from the pulpit at the Methodist Church. There was plenty of espousing on charity to freemen, even to runaways. He suspected she had suggested employing freemen from the settlements as woodchoppers. It would have been different to suggest that they work at the tannery in town. Out here, out of sight was out of mind. Now he wondered about

Hannibal's statement: "You do not want to see too much." Could the new hands be runaways? Was his father knowingly hiding runaways and giving them a means of support? Would he sell land to a freeman? Exchange for labor? He knew that his father did not let good deals pass lightly.

He hopped to his feet and brushed his pants. He shook Hannibal's hand, "I will give your report to Pa and pass your idea on to Ma. You and the men have a grand Independence Day! See you in the morning. This is my last run today."

Hannibal smiled broadly, "And you enjoy yours, Young Master Grant. Not too much mischief now. Thank Mistress Grant for all of us! Kiss all the girls at the fair!"

Ulysses had a lot to think about on the slow trip into town. How many loads of timber in twenty acres, how much bark? Were runaways working in his father's woods? What would happen to his family if they were discovered? Would Hannibal do all of the stump removal himself, or does he plan to hire one of the men to work with him? Would Lucy be waiting? Could he persuade her to go to her Aunt Betsy's ?

"Atta girl, Molly. Keep it up Jake. It's a short day's work today. Just pay no attention to those cannon blasts tonight."

Cincinnati

The *Aurora's* steam whistle sounded a long mournful tone. The pilot placed his paddlewheel into reverse. The paddles beat the water to froth. The boat, heading downriver directly into the late afternoon sun, drifted with the current. Passengers crowded the starboard side of the hurricane deck to gain a glimpse of their destination. Roustabouts on the main deck readied cargo for unloading. Two quick whistle blasts and two rings of the massive brass bell signaled to the Covington Ferry to make way for the *Aurora* to maneuver.

The pilot ordered, "Ready to come about!" He let his vessel skim just below the lower end of the Cincinnati Landing. "Come about!" Bells dinged. The paddlewheel went into hard forward. Rudders put her into a quick turn causing timbers and planks to shudder. Passengers made their way to the port side. The pilot waited, waited and watched for the moment that experience dictates. "Easy to!" More bells. The churning paddlewheel eased; the rudders straightened. The steamboat glided towards an opening along the landing and nestled between the *Patriot* and the *General Pike*.

Hiram Ulysses Grant, perched on a tobacco barrel at the top of the public landing, watched until the *Aurora* was tied fast to its chosen position in the long line of steamers, now an even two dozen. He picked up his pad and continued sketching a pencil likeness of the *General Pike*, the largest and fanciest vessel along the bank. It was a vision of white posts, rails, arches, and gingerbread from stem to stern, from waterline to pilothouse. Green and gold accents, ornate lettering, and lofty black smokestacks made the sidewheeler a wonder not only to boys, but to all who beheld her.

Lyss had what was left of the day to himself. He would leave early the next day for home. He had brought a load of harness leather to Parker Livery and Warehouse on the riverfront. His father and Mr. Parker had been doing business for several years. Maybe that is what made his father stand out from other tanners. Not satisfied with local trade, he was continually seeking bigger and better markets. Parker was not only a customer, but also a jobber supplying harness to smaller liveries. The entrepreneur also ran drays and rented carriages. Lyss' team was stabled in Parker's four-story brick building. His wagon was also inside the building, loaded with five packs of pigskins, three barrels of salt, a keg of sulfur, and two fancy saddles to be hauled to Georgetown in payment for the load of harness.

Lyss was a bit of a businessman himself. On this trip he had hired out his extra wagon space to deliver to the city market two barrels of dried apples. He was keeping a hopeful eye out here at the landing for anything to carry back on his return trip. One article he would carry free of charge had not yet arrived at Parker's: a case of twelve hymnals for the Methodist Church. He thought it strange that he, out of all of the people of Georgetown, should be taking hymnals to town. Music, church or otherwise, definitely was not his inclination. He could not tell one note from another. He categorized music under "nuisance."

Though his fourteenth birthday was a little over two months past, the lad already had learned many tricks of freight hauling. The key to the trip ahead lay in calculating the weight he could pull up the hill from Cincinnati's East Side bottoms to the Bethel Pike and also up Long Hill from White Oak Creek to the environs of Georgetown. April rains require good judgment when fording the creek. The steep descent ahead of the creek necessitates patient preparation. He planned to chain the right rear wheel to the frame. He would then fasten an iron boot for the wheel to slide on. Finally he would use long chains to drag a log behind his rig. Thus braked he would begin his slow steady decline. As for Bethel Pike, it was one of the best roads in the region, easily passable even in April. At Sugartree Trail a bit east of Bantam he would detour south a half mile to Grandma and Grandpa Simpson's farm. A portion of the vast six hundred acre spread actually abutted Bethel Pike. The stately brick home and grand outbuildings displayed prosperity beyond the norm for the region. Grandma Sarah Simpson was his favorite relative. Always congenial, thoughtful, always with an interesting comment, she doted on her grandchildren. She always prepared Ulysses' favorite foods, remembering that he never ate chicken or other foul, tame or wild. She seemed to always have fruit pie coming out of the oven, no matter the season. Ulysses could not help but consider the contrast between her warm outgoing countenance and the practicality of his mother. Of course his mother's maladies, recurring harsh headaches, had to be taken into account. And it was a natural fact, Sarah was his mother's step-mother.

He intended an early start in the morning to arrive at the Simpsons in time to stable his horses and help with barnyard chores before dark. The following day he could easily complete the trip home. He would be joined by little sisters Clara and Virginia who had ridden along in his wagon to Grandma Simpson's on Saturday's outbound trip. There they stayed while he had continued to Cincinnati on Monday.

Ulysses added a detail to his drawing's forecastle. He drew in two flags atop. A gentleman in a grey suit looked over his shoulder and studied.

"Splendid rendering," the man said. "Could I employ you to make me one?"

Lyss replied, "This one is yours for two bits."

"Deal!"

Lyss felt privileged to fall into good fortune. As he was wont to do, he decided to have dinner at a hotel as a reward. He moved to a keg and reviewed the city's bustling waterfront once more. Here the steady incline of the cobblestoned riverbank gave good mooring no matter the river's height – low water to flood stage. The "Landing" was open public space from Parker's to nearly a half mile downstream. Up behind him where the bank leveled, the city began. Front Street was lined with two and three-story, some four, commercial buildings. Traveling inward two and three blocks deep from Front Street, the city boasted columned churches and public buildings along with stately hotels and banks. The growing city reached north in a horseshoe shape to the base of majestic hills. Cincinnati owed its superior commerce to its landing, and it knew it. That and old Fort Washington.

Fort Washington had been demolished more than thirty years earlier, well before the War of 1812. When built as a wilderness outpost beside a small burgh, it protected early settlers north of the Ohio River. At least it tried to. Early campaigns by Josiah Harmar and Arthur St. Clair were severely beaten back by the Miami, Shawnee, Delaware and allied tribes under the acclaimed Chief Little Turtle. Until Anthony Wayne's campaign north from here to the Maumee River, tribes continued to raid the countryside to within sight of the fort. It was Governor St. Clair who named the town after the heroic Cincinnatus who, forsaking political ambition, returned to his country farm after leading the Roman Legion to great victories.

The fort grounds had been plowed asunder in the rush towards commercial progress. Before heading up to Fifth Street for supper at the Dennison House, Ulysses poked around looking for remnants that might be seen. He inquired of local shopkeepers as to the location. "Is there anything left of the old fort to see?" "Do you know the location?" "Are there any local stories about the fort?" All to no avail. The slate had been wiped clean. Only written accounts of great events remained. Grandma Sarah Simpson kept the old stories alive. A voracious reader, she had an insatiable appetite for history, particularly history of her young country. These stories she tenderly imparted to her children and grandchildren.

Evening brought a subdued hubbub to the Landing by the time Ulysses returned. Loading and unloading of crates and barrels and trunks subsided. Deckhands and stevedores finished tasks without their usual shouting. Drovers headed the last of the livestock to unseen destinations. Mobs of hurried passengers gave way to fine clothed gentlemen escorting gowned ladies on the Front Street promenade. The river shone with a brief purple hue from the departing sun, then gained a faint sheet of silver from a low crescent moon. High upon the top decks of several boats, windows revealed soft yellow-orange lamplight. From behind, Ulysses could hear banjo music and laughter drifting from Harold's Tavern. Banjo strumming was one form of music that he could relate to.

The clop, clop, clop of horses' hooves and the grinding rattle of steel rimmed wheels rolling over cobblestones reminded him to tend to his mission. An early start demanded early to bed. He strolled upstream to Parker's. There he had his choice of bunking with the teamsters and warehouse hands, or bedding down with the horses. He chose the cleaner of the two: the stable with fresh straw and his own bedroll. Except for the hymnals, his load was ready for the morning. The office had closed while he was out, so he would need to check the hymnal status in the morning. He inspected his team to see that all was well situated, then made his bed. His head filled with the drone of street traffic, interrupted sporadically with shouts and laughter from the card game upstairs. He drifted off wondering about what Grandma Simpson and the girls were baking.

It seemed to Ulysses that the card game was getting boisterous with unreasonable shouting and banging. How could he sleep with such commotion? He tried to remember the banjo tune to sooth himself back to sleep. Banjo music was not something he would hear in Georgetown. The shouting was getting louder.

"Outrageous! What skullduggery are they up to?" Lyss wondered half aloud.

A bundle of men poured into the stable, knocking over water pails in the process. Ulysses pulled his blanket over his head.

"You boys out the back way to the loading dock!" It was Parker's office manager, Harvey. "Head upstream and hide in the brush along the bank! Stay hidden all night if need be! Don't poke your head out for nothing. I'll come around when it's all clear. Git now!"

Ulysses sat up, discombobulated at the shenanigans.

Harvey continued with orders, "Shep, bust up that old barrel and pass the staves around. The rest of you grab some axes and pitchforks. Post yourselves at the front entrance. Show that we mean business!"

George Parker burst in, "They're comin' down Broadway! No time to lose! Are all the freemen out? Pete, help Grant harness up his team. I want him out of here. Grant! Grant my boy!" Parker quickly stepped to Ulysses and shook his shoulder, "Get your wagon ready! I don't want to be responsible for you! Hitch up! I'll be right back!" Parker headed for his office.

Shep, a giant stable hand, moved Ulysses' team to his wagon. He threw horse collars at Ulysses.

Lyss jumped up. Through a window he could see men with torches jostling down the street. He threw Shep a puzzled look. Shep was scurrying about like a squirrel, uncommon for the big man.

Lyss, "Don't agitate the horses, Shep! We'll never get them harnessed if you excite them. What's the commotion? It can't be morning already."

Shep, "Boss says to get you out of here, posthaste! The Irish are riled up! They've been threatening trouble for weeks. Now trouble it is! Here, you do the bits. I'll get the singletrees."

Ulysses fetched a feed bucket. He turned it upside down to use for a stool to reach the horses' heads. His voice soothed the skittish horses while his hands effortlessly went about their task. He knew the story. The growing population, Irish and others, blamed the freemen for lack of employment. They threatened to drive them out of town, burn them out if need be. Violence had erupted seven years earlier when a mob drove half the blacks out of town. Now mob mentality had burst forth again. Parker's Livery could be a target. All the warehouses customarily employed freemen.

Harvey called inside, "They've turned downstream – word is to the West End bottoms! Stay alert, though, you can't predict malcontents."

Lyss fastened the final hame strap. He made a circuit to adjust the check chains. All was ready.

George Parker came up and shoved a leather pouch into his hands, "Take this! There's three hundred fifty dollars in there. Take it to your Pa for advance credit." He turned away.

Lyss, "Do you have some paper for me? What about the hymnals?"

Parker, "Ha! This is no time for receipts, nor for hymnals! You father will understand." Parker gathered himself and slowed down, "Listen to me. Take the low road directly to East End. Don't stop for nothing. Just keep your head down and keep moving as quickly as you can. Keep going until you are well past East End, then you will be alright. I just can't have you here if that mob comes back. Your father would never forgive me. You'll just have to make do the best you can in this emergency. You just keep a wide berth of any goings-on. I'll have two boys run along aside for a ways to see you off. I have to go now."

With that George Parker turned and left. Ulysses understood – he had his mission. Mr. Parker had confidence in his abilities to carry it out. Quick action was the theme! He placed his right foot on the front wheel hub and resolutely climbed to the seat. He unhooked a latch and placed the pouch in a hidden compartment in the bottom of the wagon seat. He nodded to Harvey that he was ready.

Harvey led the team to the stable door. He called out, "Is it all clear out there?"

"All clear!" came the reply.

Harvey, "Open up! Boss says to send two runners with him a ways."

The door opened. Ulysses peered onto the dim street. He said a quick prayer, "Lord, don't let me run over anybody." He snapped the reins, "Step to Buck – lively now!"

The wagon jerked. His rig bounded into the street. He turned a sharp right and headed out. Out the corner of his eye he saw a band of Parker's men huddled near the main door. If any followed along he did not see them. His gaze was fixed on the street ahead. He did not want to crash into an oncoming wagon or knock over some fool standing in the street. Front Street was perfectly straight for a good way. He soon crossed the canal bridge and quickly put it behind him. He let his team have their way until the street angled to the right to drop down to the river's edge.

"Easy Buck, not so fast now. You've had your way. Let's ease up for awhile. It's going to be a long night."

Lyss then realized that he had no idea what time it was. Had he been asleep at all, a short while, all night? Was it midnight yet, or near dawn? What about breakfast? The rumble of the wheels softened when the cobblestone turned to dirt. The silence had a calming effect. Occasionally a wheel hit a rock and sent a report that seemed to roll across the river and back. He planned ahead. He would silently move through Fulton and ascend the hill. Above he would find a secluded spot to stop and wait for dawn. Then he would find a farmstead where he could procure some feed and water for the animals and perhaps some food for himself.

Lights appeared ahead through the brush. The little community was lit up. As he drew closer he could see that some of the lights were moving. He had no options. There was only one way through, to plunge straight ahead. What should anybody care about a boy and a wagon, strange as it may be at this time of night, whatever time it was?

"Pup-pup, come on now, pup-pup." The horses went into a steady trot. "Pay attention, now. Keep it up!"

Some men were standing in front of a tin shop. They looked him over as he rumbled past. Farther along two men with torches challenged him.

"Who goes there?" "Hold up, you!" "You haulin' anybody in there? Stop and let me take a look!" "Stop I say!"

Ulysses headed his team directly towards the man on the right.

The man on the left called, "Watch it, Pat!" The other dodged, slipped, and fell to the street. "For the love of God, boy, you could have killed him!"

He threw his torch at the wagon. It bumped off the side and slid under the left rear wheel. Ulysses felt the bump yet kept his pace, looking neither left nor right.

Behind he heard, "You alright, Pat? You break a leg? Somebody help us here! I'll get you for this, you crazy farmer!"

The pace was kept past the last shed and on into the countryside. At the Little Miami River bridge he eased up and crossed over. He knew where to find a turnout. Though unsure about possible pursuers, he thought it best to water his horses. They could use a spell before the hill challenge. "Wait here, boys. Take a breather." He scurried down to the river and dipped his felt hat. What moon there was disappeared behind thick clouds. By the time he was underway again a downpour erupted. Lightning began to play; thunder grumbled. Not the best conditions for driving a team up a steep hill: complete darkness; driving rain; glaring lightning; nervous horses. But forge ahead he must. He needed more distance between him and the fanatical town.

He took the left road to begin the ascent. Progress was slow. Only intermittent lightning illuminated the course. The storm turned the road into a rapidly flowing stream.

The horses began to balk at the task. Lyss did not know how near the summit may be. Twice Buck stumbled and caught himself. The undertaking became precarious. Lyss knew that he would need to act swiftly to avoid losing control and having the rig careen back to the bottom. He applied the brake – enough to hold things in place only briefly.

In a firm voice Lyss commanded, "Whoa, guys! Hold

up! Whoa, stay steady."

He freed the reins and released the brake. He leaped from the seat.

"Quickly," he thought to himself, "and don't you dare stumble."

He reached for Buck's rump and, grabbing the harness, pulled himself along uphill. He gave Buck a quick pat on the snout. Digging his boots firmly into the mire, he gave a solid tug on the lead line.

Calmly, but masterfully, he said, "Here we go now. Steady. Up and out of here."

Thankfully it was only a few steps to the crest. A few more steps and he stopped to rest. Lightning streaked wildly. Lyss was soaked and exhausted. A few deep breaths then wearily he continued to lead on foot. Onward he drudged. He lunged one step at a time. The rain whipped first from the left then from the right. It was difficult to determine the road.

Not far ahead a light flickered. Again. He made out a man tending a fire, no easy trick in this storm. He turned off the road towards the light. "Ahoy there in camp!"

A voice returned, "Who's yer?"

Lyss, "Grant from Georgetown, seeking shelter!"

The voice, "Wall, bring your rig in. Tie up to that big red oak." Was Lyss supposed to identify trees in a dark downpour? "This is a good stand of timber. Don't worry about falling limbs. Not unless we get a direct hit. I've used this camp a number of times. Tie up and come on over."

Lyss made out a huckster's wagon with winged

tarps in front and on the side. "I'd be much obliged if I could duck under your canopy. I'm as wet as a rag mop."

The voice was friendly, "Why, gracious sakes, you're jist a boy. What ya doin' out here? You come up that hill?"

"Yes sir." Lyss replied. "I had no choice. I was bound for Bethel in the morning, then on to Georgetown. But there was trouble in Cincinnati and I was rushed out of town."

"Trouble, you say. Well, I'm not surprised. That town has been a tempest ready to boil over. I should of left earlier yesterday and been well along. But I overstayed my time at O'Malley's and got a late start. A man has got to have some fun for himself now and then, don't ya agree? Well, things were getting testy at O'Malley's and I skedaddled. Yanks say there's too many Irish taking all the jobs. The Irish blame the freemen for all their woes. On and on it goes. Talk got pretty rough and I didn't want any part of it. Name's Oppenheim, Levi Oppenheim. A peddler by trade. Just got stocked up and heading out on my rounds. Grant you say? Georgetown? You relation to the tanner Grant?"

Lyss, "Jesse Grant is my Pa. I made a delivery to Cincinnati and am on my return."

Levi, "You look a might young for that." Lightning cracked nearby – close enough to startle a mummy. The pair instinctively ducked. "Wow! Close enough." They both chuckled at how they had jumped. "I'll get you a tin cup so you can warm up with some coffee. Want a blanket? I've plenty."

Lyss, "Yes and yes, thank you."

Levi reached into the wagon with a hand that knew every inch of merchandise within. "There you are, son. Now let me see. Grant, Georgetown, yes, yes. Your Pa likes fine clothes. Your Ma is frugal and likes things plain. A devout woman, if there ever was one. Got to admire her for that. She doesn't buy trinkets or fluff. Practical stuff, well made, sturdy, that's her. Doesn't go in for the newest kitchen gadget. For most homes, that's usually my lead-in. Something special for the kitchen that the lady can't find at the mercantile. Pearl buttons or a pocket knife for a gift gets their attention. Something extravagant that they wouldn't buy in public. Seems your Ma purchased a parlor lamp with a rose motif last time. That's extravagant for her!" He paused for a sip, then continued, "Which of Grant's boys are you? You the one I saw riding lickety-split bareback on a horse along the town square, standing up on its back on one foot?"

Lyss expressed chagrin, "Yah, that would be me. I don't do that anymore. Ma thinks it's showing off, so I don't do it. I only used to do it to show that the horse was well trained to pace. They say that I have a knack for training pacers."

Levi, "Why, I should say so. You're famous wider than you know. Yes, indeed. The boy that understands horses and horses understand the boy. If and when we get some sun, I'd like you to look over my pony – see if you have any suggestions. Right now, I'll lean back here and get some sleep. You make yourself a warm spot and rest up. What did ya say your given name is?"

Lyss, "Ulysses. Hiram Ulysses Grant."

Ulysses dozed off almost before he got it said.

To Covington

Ulysses would not be home for the biggest horse auction of the year. That was of little concern to the fifteen year old as he eyed the steamer before him. Light grey smoke drifted from its smokestacks. The *Clarion* was a mid-sized sternwheeler. Tied parallel to the Ripley wharf it looked huge. Pristine white with red trim and gold accents, it was a regular visitor to the Ohio town. One could take her upriver to Marietta or down to Louisville. On special trips she went up as far as Pittsburgh. Though now pointed upstream, she was loading for the downward trip.

A skinny lad with fiery red hair was chirping orders in a high voice to roustabouts loading boiler wood. "Hardwood here, hardwood here, hardwood here, pitch pine yonder, pitch pine yonder, hardwood here, hardwood here, hardwood here. Hold it! You should know better! We don't want that cottonwood! Tell them any more of that and we will pitch the whole shootin' match overboard!" He continued the process, "Next up!

[43]

Start a new rick over here."

Observing all the loading proceedings, Ulysses sat next to the wharf on bales of leather he and cousin Johnny had unloaded from their wagon before noon. Johnny had long departed. Lyss had been to Ripley and its wharf often in the past. He had sailed in skiffs out into the river and over to Kentucky. He had seen paddleboats of all sizes come and go. But this one was special. This one he would ride to Louisville – his first trip on a real riverboat. He would be the envy of all the kids in Georgetown. Actually, he already was to most of them who had never traveled more than five miles from home.

Lyss regularly made trips to surrounding counties. Cincinnati was familiar to him. He had driven wagons and buggies far up into Ohio and down into Kentucky. Only the Walker boys had traveled farther. Answering invitations by the Mexican government, their family had homesteaded in Texas, only to return after two years. Not to be outdone, Jesse Grant concocted a trip to New Orleans two years ago. Searching for business opportunities, he ventured up the Red River to Natchitoches, Louisiana and on to the town of Nacogdoches in the province of Texas.

Lyss' favorite drive was the rugged narrow winding road leading down along White Oak Creek Canyon to the Ohio River at Higginsport. That little burgh boasted a landing of its own with enough freight and passengers to provide Ulysses a regular business. On his last trip he brought up three young ladies wearing high fashion. He laughed, quietly, as they shrieked while thrice crossing the swollen creek.

The lad on the *Clarion*, hardly a year older than Lyss, looked up. He called to Lyss, "Hey you! What you got in them bales?"

Lyss replied, "Finished leather – from machinery belting to the finest pigskin for furniture, property of Jesse Grant of Georgetown."

The lad, "Where ya bound for?"

Lyss, "Through to Louisville."

Lad, "You got papers yet?"

Lyss held high up over his head what the purser had given him.

Lad, "Well, jist you don't let nary a stevedore touch them bales until everything else is loaded and in place." He turned his attention, "That's enough pitch pine, no more." He pointed, "Fill in with hardwood up to that post." He surveyed stern to stem. "Oh, Lordy. They're loading goats." He bounded over to the pens, "Farmer man, push that gate in tight. We don't want any goats getting loose. They'd likely stick their necks under the thrust rod. What a bloody mess we'd have!"

The goat farmer gave the boy a look of aggravation as if to say, "You telling me how to handle goats?" His countrified gentrification corralled his tongue.

The boy called to a hand, "Tevia! Tevia, make a hole in front of the pens for them bales that boy is sittin' on. One layer of hogsheads with the bales put up on top. Leave room above for him to nest." He returned his attention to the wood, "Enough, men. That's enough boiler wood. Any more and we'd be tripping over it." He gave a shrill whistle to gain the purser's attention. He signaled that the job was complete and the vendor could be paid accordingly.

He called to Ulysses, "Now, boy, let's get them bales aboard. Tevia, get some help and see to it proper."

Lyss pulled his rucksack over his shoulder and followed the stevedores up the plank. His merchandise was efficiently stowed where the boy had directed. Lyss climbed the stack and perched atop.

The boy watched his motions, "Your first trip, right?"

Lyss, "Yes, sir. First time on a real steamer!"

Lad, "Name's Patrick. No 'sir' necessary. You can come down. No need to ride up there permanent. Your wares will stay dry there. You'll still have a good breeze atop fer sleepin'. And your bales will be out of the way. Ya won't be bothered 'till Louisville. You've got the run of the boiler deck the whole way. You can depart at the ports, jist be aboard at shove-off." He turned away, then back, "You got a gun or knife in that sack?"

Lyss, "No, sir. Just a pocket knife for general use."

Patrick, "Well, if you got any valuables you'll need to keep an eye on them yourself. Don't leave them lay around."

Lyss, "Thanks, I will follow your advice."

Patrick, "You got food enough?"

Lyss, "I do, thank you, ham, cornbread, and honey. Plus some fresh cherries."

Patrick, "Good. More'n I need to know."

The purser, now aboard, directed Patrick to the fore.

They huddled and shuffled papers. The purser pulled some small ropes; bells dinged in the pilothouse – three dings, repeat.

A long mournful blast erupted from the steam whistle. The *Clarion's* brass bell clanged. The purser headed down the gangplank and removed a barrier chain. Two men, apparently father and son, shuffled up the plank to the boiler deck. They stashed their bags then searched for a comfortable area to lounge. A gentleman and two ladies made their way up and mounted the grand staircase to the stateroom deck. Their luggage followed in the arms of two deckhands.

The purser ran up the swinging gangway. He pulled his bell ropes – this time four dings, repeated. The steam whistle shook the valley with two longs, a short, and an extra long deafening bellow. The big brass bell clanged a cadence. A thick mooring line to the fore was untied from a huge cottonwood tree and slung to the deck. A deckhand deftly arranged it on the cavel. The aft line was heaved to. Some bells dinged a chorus. Hands swung the gangway in and stowed it securely in place. The smokestacks belched thick and black; the huge paddlewheel came to life. A moment of creaking and quaking, then slowly the vessel drifted backward and away from the little wharf. The wheel quickened. Steady the steamer held, then lunged forward. Upstream and out to the channel she went. Two blasts and two bells, she rounded to. Ulysses was underway! Only adventure lay ahead!

Lyss stood as far forward as he could muster. He

watched the familiar town of Ripley fade away. He took
in the full view. The forest rode steep hills up from the
water's edge on the left and on the right. The mighty
Ohio lay before him. He stood motionless, silently
watching for familiar landmarks. Everything blended
into the forest.

In preparation, he had studied river charts. He
planned to observe every river port along the entire
route. He waited to catch a view of Higginsport.

Impatience got the better of him. The engineering of
the steam engine, the paddle thrusters, the rudder,
everything about the mechanics of the boat was too
inviting. A sense of freedom was overwhelming. The
beauty of the landscape was overpowering. He tried to
take it all in at once. There was too much. He would need
to take each in turn. He had seen steam engines earlier:
two on saw mills and one at a furniture shop. The
scenery would last through to the end.

He decided to investigate the power transfer from
the engine to the paddle wheel. Back and forth, up and
down, around went rods and shafts. He watched a
mechanic begin his rounds with a grease bucket. All was
mystifying, bewildering. Ulysses glanced up from this
baffling contraption just in time to catch a glimpse of the
unmistakable mouth of White Oak Creek. Quickly
Higginsport came into view, at least what could be seen
from the middle of the Ohio River. Lyss was
disappointed to see what little significance the town bore
upon the river. A few rooftops, the blacksmith shop, and
the path to the landing were all that could be discerned.

The barge that served as the town pier could scarcely be seen. The flag was up, indicating downward bound cargo to be had. The *Clarion* ignored the port, leaving its commerce to smaller vessels. Swiftly they passed. Higginsport melted into the unending trees. His "home port" was of inconsequence to all on board except him. He wondered if the town was even on the captain's charts.

The *Clarion* moved to the larboard and put in at Augusta. A small upbound packet pulled out only minutes before their approach. The town filled a low plain between the river and the Kentucky hills. It continued to prosper despite recent floods. It was a quick stop. Four sleek horses were boarded along with kegs of whiskey and tobacco – no passengers. Patrick directed actions on the main deck. The flurry of activity over, the paddlewheel backed the boat to catch the swift flow.

Lyss made another circuit of the deck. The rhythm of the steam engine was clicking in his head. He tapped his thigh with the tips of his fingers in cadence. He began to study the cargo. Nothing unusual, same materials as he had seen at Cincinnati, Higginsport, and Ripley. The port of Moscow was unceremoniously passed by. He decided to concentrate on the north bank to pick out Point Pleasant, the village where he was born. His family had moved to Georgetown after his first birthday. He had since been to the isolated community only once. Though small, the public landing was of good size. The landing's smooth uphill slope provided good mooring at all river levels.

Patrick interrupted Ulysses' thoughts, "Ya git settled in? Here, catch!" He tossed Ulysses one of a pair of peaches. "Things'll settle down for awhile, now. Nothing happening 'till Covington. We've bales of hemp to unload there. Captain says we'll moor there for the night, just up the Licking River from the point."

Lyss had viewed the area from the Cincinnati Landing. He replied, "I've been to Cincinnati a number of times – watched the traffic at the point."

Patrick advised, "Captain Hendricks don't like to pull into Cincinnati in the dim light of dusk. Says he witnessed a collision a couple of years back. The *Polander* rammed the *Hornet* in an evening fog. Captain of the *Hornet* was crushed dead on the spot – lots of others injured, not to mention the repair costs. The captain of the *Polander* was dismissed by the company."

Ulysses winced at the image of colliding steamers. He envisioned other legendary wrecks up and down the river. Even General Lafayette during his grand tour of the continent twelve years previous was not exempt. He had to swim to the Indiana shore to survive a sinking sidewheeler.

Patrick inquired, "I don't see many boys my age shepherding freight. You a relative of the tanner?"

Lyss, "I'm Jesse Grant's first son. My brothers work the tannery; I'm always out and about doing this or that."

Patrick, "What kind of 'that'?"

Lyss, "Well, a tannery can't run without bark. Oak is best, but we use a variety, whatever is available. I haul in the bark, fetch in the firewood, bring quicklime. I transport finished goods to surrounding towns, sometimes to Cincinnati. In the process, I've developed a little freighting business. This summer I've been hauling timber to town for building a new jailhouse. Next year I hope to do the farming, enough grain to feed our horses and some to sell."

Patrick, "Sounds like you're a busy guy."

Lyss, "What I'm good at is breaking horses, draft horses plus pacers for buggies. Not much money in that, though." He spotted Point Pleasant, "Look, I was born in that town, Point Pleasant they call it. Lived in Georgetown all my life except that first year."

Patrick, "Tell me about Georgetown. I see all the ports, but don't get up the hill at all. Don't know much about the interior of your state. From what they bring to the wharfs, Ohio must be all trees and pigs. Must be some tobacco fields and grain, I guess. I've never been on a farm, don't know much about farm animals. Some of the hands were debatin' whether goats can swim – I have no idea."

Lyss was intrigued with the boy. "Georgetown has progress enough. We're the county seat with a public square, court house, old jail, lawyers, our own newspaper, a pair of mercantiles, two smithies, and of course the tannery. Now there's a meat packer. Georgetown has a fine new brick school. Students attend by subscription, January through March. There is a grist mill to the east and one to the west. We have the Masons, a debating society, a dramatic club, four churches. As for goats, well, I don't recall ever seeing one swim. From what I've seen, they seem to have an aversion to water in general."

Patrick, "I see, you're proud of your town – a place to belong."

Lyss, "Yeh, I reckon so. Why not?" He pitched the peach pit into the river. "Thanks for the peach. Good flavor it was." He hopped onto some grain sacks, "Where do you hail from?"

Patrick turned his back momentarily, then faced Ulysses. "I'll tell you, but you can't repeat any of this, right?"

Ulysses nodded the affirmative.

Patrick took a deep breath, "Well, here goes. My Pa, older brother, and I were working the Virginy coal mines. Pa and Mick got caught in a pocket of gas. Mick died right out. Pa got out, but couldn't work any longer. It wasn't long until he was in debtor's prison. I asked to be switched to the night crew. The second night I lit out for the river, built a raft and drifted along. Rode the river clear down to Parkersburg. Stowed aboard the *Clarion*, been here ever since. Captain Hendricks threatened to take me back, said I was surely an indenture. Not true, mind you. Well, he never did take me back, you can see, and never will. He gave me a family name of 'Yeoman.' I'm Patrick Yeoman now. I can read and cipher, so he let me apprentice under the purser. Someday I'll be cub pilot, you can bet on that. When the river ices up, the Captain is going to school me at Marietta to hone my skills. That's where he is out of. This boat has one captain and the one captain is the one pilot. It's jist like it's his own boat, though a Marietta syndicate holds the papers on her."

Patrick emphasized "syndicate", not knowing for sure its meaning, but it sounded important.

Lyss, "Obviously the Captain has given you responsibilities, just like my Pa with me. Responsibilities are earned, though. I refuse to work in the tannery, so I work hard to wipe out my Pa's disappointment."

Ulysses took in the river scenery for a moment. "You don't know, Patrick, but you're the envy of every boy in Georgetown, probably every boy within twenty miles of the river down its whole length."

"How so?"

Lyss, "Ha! All boys want to be a boatman! Plying the rivers to far off places, clear to New Orleans even, that's the dream."

Patrick, "Yeh, sometimes I forget. I haven't been lower than the falls at Louisville. Captain Hendricks says one day we'll go the length, though. His license is for the Ohio only. They have separate pilot requirements for the Upper Mississippi and separate for the Lower Mississippi. One day, I'll have all three, I tell you. Anyway, I got it good and I know it. I'll make the best of it. I jist see myself as a stone skipping on a pond. I reckon I'm on my third bounce."

Lyss pondered the analogy, "A lot of people would be better off if they would just make the best of where they are. So many are looking for something that's not there, expecting stars to intervene or something."

Patrick hopped up and stretched, "Can I get you

some food from the galley. I've got free rein."

Lyss, "No, thank you. I am well set. Mrs. Bailey, the doctor's wife just up the hill from us, she made a big fuss about me leaving. She sent treats enough."

Patrick, "As I said, keep watch on your valuables. The river brings out the best in some people, but in others the worst. Don't trust anybody on the river. Let them talk, but be a slow listener."

New Richmond was far behind; Cincinnati could not be far ahead. Ulysses sat forward near the prow and listened to the water ripple. With each breath he inhaled freedom. Occasional sprays of fine mist drifted over the deck providing a cooling effect against the August doldrums. Behind him within the boiler deck the engines were mustering their own considerable heat. The spray, the breeze, the lapping water were refreshing. The view was magical. Surprisingly, he could feel the pat-pat-pat-pat of the waterwheel from the opposite end of the boat. His mind drifted to thoughts heretofore unknown. What if he accomplished his mission and then, instead of returning home, what if he built a raft and followed wherever the river led into the hinterlands? He could spend his years roving hither and yon. Maybe he could earn some money and secure passage on a huge Mississippi boat. Perhaps Patrick could teach him enough that he could become a deckhand on a downward bound vessel. He had always been told that he was good at arithmetic. Maybe he could even be engaged in a pilothouse high atop a pristine paddleboat. His brain grew giddy at the possibilities.

A thump woke him from his stupor. A floating tree trunk skidded alongside the hull. To the starboard he saw the Little Miami River emptying into the Ohio. Behind he could see the hill where peril was a step away during the cloudburst. Stories of events earlier that night had been in all the papers. Reports were that rioters had burned out at least a dozen homes at West End. Newspaper offices were smashed. Businesses that catered to freemen were systematically wrecked. Hundreds of black families have since packed off to other environs.

Patrick, mimicking a town crier, tromped about the boiler deck calling to his charges, "Hear Ye! An announcement from the Captain! We will tie up for the night at Covington. No loading or unloading of freight will take place until daylight tomorrow morning. Passengers on all decks may debark. Return to the ship by ten o'clock if you wish to return for the night. No one may come aboard after ten o'clock. Cincinnati bound passengers may ferry over this evening, or wait for us to cross over tomorrow, likely by noon. That is all!"

Ulysses watched ahead as the Covington point steadily approached. When it seemed that he could reach out and touch the bank, the boat swung to the larboard into the channel of the Licking River. A few yards more and they made landing in a cool spot hidden from the lingering sun. He now had the opposite view of what he had seen so often from the Cincinnati Landing.

His decision was quickly made. He would stay aboard to watch over his goods.

Deck hands stood guard at each plank. People shuffled to and fro. The boiler was allowed to cool to a moderate level. Ulysses returned to his nest and fixed his supper. One of Mrs. Bailey's cakes topped it off. He wondered about Patrick. He had never contemplated having a brother or family member die. What was it like to have a home that moved about, seldom in the same place two days in a row? He would like to meet this Captain that took the boy in. River pilots were kings of their domain. Captain Hendricks must be king of the river pilots.

Evening was quiet along the Kentucky shore. Most of the small group of the *Clarion's* passengers strolled the promenade on the high bank. Patrick had bustled about then disappeared into the upper reaches of the steamer. Alone in his nest, Lyss sensed not another person on the boiler deck save one crewman keeping guard at each exit. Even the goats were gone, they being the only freight allowed off this night, much to the delight of the crew. Occasionally a passenger or crewman leisurely descended the grand staircase and wondered down the gangplank. It was tempting to go out for exercise himself. He could take in the sights while limbering his muscles. But night would soon cloak the streets in darkness and present unknown dangers. He hopped down and made a brisk walk around the deck for a few laps. Off the stern, upon the east bank of the Licking River, the last rays of the sun tinted the white buildings of Newport Barracks with a pinkish hue. He studied the steam gauges. He wondered about those who could construct such a ship.

He envisioned visiting the Marietta shipyards where she was built.

The steam whistle blew a nine-thirty warning for passengers to return aboard. Lyss revisited his makeshift bunk. At home he would have been asleep by now in preparation for an early rise. He had nothing requiring him to rise in the morning other than to take in the sights and watch the boiler being fired. At home there would have been the commotion of brother Sim and sisters Clara and Virginia plus baby Orvil and cousins and parents bedding down in close quarters. Lyss had his own room overlooking the tannery and his own bed. Lately cousin Johnny crowded a trundle into the small room. Johnny was no bother; he was simply subservient to the oldest boy of the household. He drifted off to sleep listening to the overhead footsteps of returning passengers.

Lawrenceburg Landing

Heat and humidity of the bright August day dictated a slower pace to the usual liveliness of the Cincinnati Landing. The *Clarion* occupied a choice spot in the line of fifteen paddleboats. All of *Clarion's* passengers but three were discharged. A majority of her cargo had gone up Cincinnati's long cobblestoned bank. Captain Hendricks was off to his obligatory rendezvous at the captains' club for the give-and-take of river news. Cargo bound for downriver ports was now being loaded.

Ulysses took in the activities from a different viewpoint than before. Somehow each task seemed more urgent, more personal, though he was not involved in the transactions. He had caught a glimpse of Captain Hendricks. The boat pilot was not the strapping physical specimen that Lyss had imagined. He was a short, stout man, one whose walk hinted that of a duck. Nonetheless, he carried an air of authority. He projected unsubdued confidence. The Captain walked with a purpose, politely nodding to those he met.

Ulysses yearned to tromp up to Parker's Livery and Warehouse to personally question Mr. Parker about his recollections of the riot. He also hoped to learn detailed events in town from a reliable eye-witness. However, even if Mr. Parker was in his office, which was less than probable, Lyss would likely have to wait a good while to be admitted. He simply could not leave his charge that length of time. He did, though, calculate that he could roam the Landing within sight of the boat and look for a familiar face or two. Perhaps he could find someone to exchange stories of that fateful night.

He dared not wander far, but it was against his disposition to sit idle. There was a tug-of-war in his mind between his responsibilities and the urge to explore. He decided to do a sketch of the *Clarion*. This he would keep as his personal memento. He walked to and fro; he walked up and down the embankment to find the proper angle. He arranged a small crate at his chosen vantage spot. There he sat motionless, filling his head with every detail of the vessel. A soft touch of his pencil produced a drafted outline. Structural details were meticulously developed. Impervious to inquisitive passersby he concentrated on his work. Detail built upon detail. When satisfied, he employed shading to give depth to the finished work. By adding ripples, reflection, and water splashing from the paddlewheel, he set the image into motion plying upon the river.

By the time the pencil and pad were laid to rest, the *Clarion* had received her cargo. He saw a sizeable line of passengers queued at the gangway. The purser

[59]

unhurriedly checked in each one. Porters were seeing to luggage and escorting each party up the grand staircase to their assigned stateroom. To the rear of the well-dressed crowd was a rougher sort of gaggle. Ulysses quickly assessed that the boiler deck would soon be crowded. He moved promptly to the side plank and made his way back to his provisional berth. Arranging his belongings, he marked the space as presently occupied.

Now the opportunity that he had been waiting for presented itself. He found Patrick on the port side aft.

Ulysses inquired, timidly while yet trying to be forceful, "Patrick, a question for you!"

Patrick replied nonchalantly, "Quickly, I've plenty to do afore departure."

Lyss, "Well, Patrick, I was just wondering. Do you suppose it would be alright for me to help fire the boiler?"

Patrick, with a grin, "Well, if yer sure ya want to."

Lyss, "Sure enough!"

Patrick, "Alright then, you know which one's Tevia?"

Lyss, "Yeah, lank with dark eyebrows."

Tevia was a spindly type who had passed a shade beyond the prime of life. His voice was gravelly; his speech halting.

Patrick, "You tell Tevia that I said that you were to help stoke to pay off a debt for food."

Lyss, "Thanks, Patrick. I'll see you after we're underway."

Patrick, "Good enough, but I won't have hardly any time to spare 'till dusk. You be good to Tevia, now."

Lyss nodded and headed directly for the firebox where he found the stoker willing to have an extra pair of hands. Lyss dove into his work. A scoop of slag coal followed by three armloads of pine, repeat, repeat. The fire burned white hot. Tevia quickly ascertained that his new helper could be relied upon with a minimum of direction. He wiped off his sweat and looked about. He tapped a short row of gauges and vaguely inspected overhead pipes. He halted Lyss' work awhile and had him move coal forward in the bin. Then it was back to feeding the fire. A small pop-off valve spat a hiss of steam.

Tevia waved, "Enough! Hold back! We're in good shape for push-off. You take a break. Come back when we head downstream if you'd like."

Lyss asked, "Just wondering, why the use of pitch pine when you have good hardwood. Surely you know hardwood sustains the fire."

Tevia explained, "You're nobody's fool! I guess the secret's out. Yeah, we'll switch to hardwood once we're underway. The pine mixed with the coal gives a quick heat to bring the boilers up. The other secret is, now don't cha' go tellin' all ya know, that the mixture also billows black smoke high into the air. People ashore expect a steamer to make smoke, so we give it to 'em. Kind'a showmanship, don't cha' see? Even in small ports, the townsfolk gather in while we're at their home port. We give a bit of a show when we shove off – full steam, paddle blazing, smoke and whistle, and bells ringing." He took a step back and waved his right hand overhead, "On an autumn's still morn, the pine sends an ocean of sparks twinklin' up and up, reaching to the firmament. There ya have it."

Lyss exclaimed in wonderment, "I've seen it maybe thirty times. I never suspected for an instant that there were theatrics involved."

Tevia gave his newfound helper a wink, "Well, you're good help. I'd give ya a pat on the back 'cept for my hands." He wiped his hands on his chest. "You're also the best dressed tender I've ever seen. Ha! Hope ya didn't soil your duds. Like I said, come back after we're underway. Right now I've business to tend."

Ulysses felt satisfied with himself. Yes, Ma would have scolded him for working in his good clothes, made especially for this trip. His Pa always required him to present his best when out representing the tannery. Even for deliveries to surrounding towns, cleanliness and decent clothes were requisite. Jesse, himself, always wore a suit with vest when out and about. Mother Hannah was a stickler for cleanliness even beyond his father's directives. Her children were always the tidiest in town. Lyss inspected himself then used his bandanna to touch up. He scurried through the throng of new arrivers to gain a place to plainly view the paddlewheel.

He no sooner arrived at his choice spot than the steam whistle blasted the signal to cast off. Taut lines grew slack. Lyss was now accustomed to the shouting, the bells, the whistles of making ready to leave shore.

This time he would study the motion of the wheel that gave life to the ship. Without the paddlewheel it would be just another boat. Without the paddlewheel there would be no mystery. Without the paddlewheel there would be no romance. Today was perfect. A high midday sun illuminated every detail on the red wheel. Sun rays penetrated deep into the water until eventually fading into oblivion.

The first jolt of the steam engine being engaged into reverse sent a charge through his bones. He could feel the power as the wheel slowly began to turn – power that he had helped create. Water smacked and splashed. He could feel himself slowly slipping away from the Landing. Or was the Landing slipping away from him? He felt as if he were a part of the boat. Clouds of vapors swung over his head, swirling this way and that. He breathed in the cool mist. Power built upon power, splashing turned to churning. Miniature rainbows danced above the wheel as if to proclaim the splendor of the sun. The roaring water turned to a glistening white. Now clear of the boats lining the Landing, he felt the river tugging at him with its current. Out and back the *Clarion* slipped. Bells rang. The paddle stopped. Bells rang. Lyss braced himself. A stiff jolt meant the wheel was engaged for forward thrust. The floor shook as the paddle grasped to find a hold on the river. The water boiled. Slowly the backward sweep disappeared. Beating the water with full power, each paddle blade strained to its task. Water was flying. Lyss could not detect forward motion, but unmistakably the town of Cincinnati was moving. He was under way! Quickly the Captain would bring his mighty vessel about and point downstream. Beyond this point Lyss had never been. True adventure lay ahead!

Ulysses cupped his hand and let it slowly fill with over-splash. It shone pristinely in the bright sun. Where did this water come from? From the Allegany? From the Monongahela? Did it originate at Patrick's coal mine? Did it sprinkle the grave of some long-lost soldier, killed in the wilderness during the Indian Wars? Did it come from White Oak Creek, perhaps falling as rain in Georgetown – trickling down the brook behind the tannery? Perhaps all of these were mixed together in this handful.

How many handfuls of water would it take to float the *Clarion*? How many handfuls to fill the Ohio River at Cincinnati? Together they would all flow along and eventually tumble over the falls at Louisville. They would gather waters from the Wabash, the Cumberland, the Tennessee, and the combined waters of the Missouri and Upper Mississippi rivers. Until the recent past, river traffic was almost exclusively with the flow. Now with steamboats, upriver and downriver are of little difference. How many paddleboats exist on all the rivers? His mind jumped to and fro with wonderment.

His gaze was mesmerized by the paddlewheel. His thoughts traced the origin of its might: men sweating to mine the coal or cut the timber; teamsters hauling the fuel to the docks; stevedores filling the bins; himself fueling the boiler box; fire turning water to steam; pipes conveying steam to the engine; the piston pushing the thrust beam; the cam powering the huge red wheel; paddles smashing into the water; motion. Yet more than motion, it was a circus of fascinations.

Cincinnati faded behind. Forested hills pushed high on the left and on the right. A wide sweeping left turn meant they were near North Bend. The town and its little pier were of little consequence, but somewhere up behind the hills to the north was the Symmes mansion. Grandma Simpson enjoyed telling the story how Judge Symmes' daughter Anna went behind her father's back to marry her lover, young William Henry Harrison. Harrison was then just a lieutenant out of Fort Washington, not of suitable stature for the daughter of a wealthy landowner and a judge of the Northwest Territory. Harrison was then only recently returned from Anthony Wayne's campaign into the wilderness. He had been an aide-de-camp when the couple eloped. Grandma Simpson was a great admirer of Harrison, former Governor of the Indiana Territory, Hero of the Battle of Tippecanoe, and Army General during the War of 1812. Retired from official offices, Harrison has now returned with his wife to her former home where he oversees what remains of Symmes' empire.

Ulysses missed out on a chance to meet the esteemed politician. He was to drive his father to North Bend to meet Harrison the October past. Georgetown businessmen hoped to persuade the general to back a canal proposal, but the issue fell through. Jesse Grant was openly more dismayed at losing his opportunity to meet

Governor Harrison than he was at the loss of the project. Lyss was himself disappointed at not meeting the man.

Lyss watched ahead on the right for the mouth of the Great Miami River. What he saw did not match what he had imagined. The hills gave way to a flat delta at the mouth of an apparently placid stream lazily meandering into the Ohio. Lyss knew otherwise. The Great Miami continued swift and rocky throughout its course. He knew from his map studies that the last hill on the right, for obvious reasons, was called Shawnee Lookout. The mouth of the river defined the state line leaving his home state behind. Only two miles more and the town of Lawrenceburg appeared on the Indiana shore.

The *Clarion* deftly swung to the floating wharf. Lyss' curiosity about the town led him promptly down the gangway.

Patrick called after him, "Don't be long! Just a couple of passengers coming aboard. Be quick or be left behind!"

Lyss took a quick inventory of the two passengers, each with a small valise. A tall smartly-dressed gentleman led a fine riding horse with crafted saddle and saddlebags. His boots, though plain, showed fine workmanship. His horse was to Lyss' liking, one he would take for a ride given the opportunity. The other fellow wore a tan suit with brown trim, matching hat, and a gold vest. The trim on the suit and hat was a tad frazzled; his boots had little wear left in them. Long flowing hair was tied behind with a black ribbon. The first man's face was pale and serious; the second's was tanned and showed an easy smile. The first man's air said he's legitimate; the second not so much.

Lyss strode to the top of the landing for a gander at the town. Behind a row of clapboard homes he found a street lined with federal style brick buildings. To his right was a handsome two-story structure signed "Jesse Hundt Hotel." To his left, at the end of the street, was Vance College. He had read about the college and hoped for a visit, but he didn't dare take the time. He assessed Lawrenceburg as clean and orderly, likely to prosper.

He pulled himself away from exploring and turned back towards the boat. He had a duty to his mission of safely conducting tannery goods to their intended destination. As always for him, responsibility trumped pleasure.

Ulysses took up a position on a coil of rope at the bow. He began trying to reconnoiter directions by the position of the late afternoon sun. After a straight hop down the river, the new settlement of Aurora sat nestled in a little valley at the head of a sharp left turn. No stopping here for the *Clarion*. Giant rafts of timber tied to the bank revealed a thriving lumber business. The Ohio River glided onward through a valley of fertile fields. Around another bend and another town appeared, again on the Indiana shoreline.

Patrick trotted up, "Lyss, we'll be putting in for the night at Rising Sun. We always take on vegetables for the galley here. We'll order tonight and they will be loaded in the morning. We get cheese here, too – mighty tasty. We'll be loaded and gone right after daylight."

Lyss, "That way we will be able to see the rising sun

at Rising Sun."

Patrick, "Yeh, I never thought of it that way. I never thought of these Germans as having a sense of humor. Anyway, wait for me and I'll take you down to the boatyards. This is one of the places they make these steamboats. There was a keel and hull laid out last time through."

Lyss, "Now that I'd like more than anything. Besides, I promised myself to inspect each and every town. I'm naturally curious about new surroundings, and besides, you never know what prospects the future will present."

Patrick, "Yes, you are a curious one. I will see that you are back aboard for some vegetable soup tonight. The cook uses up all the old vegetables, puts in a little meat and serves up more than anyone can eat. Besides, you earned it with your labor. If you want, I can find an apron and you can help fire up in the morning."

Lyss, "You're on on all counts."

Patrick, "Captain Hendricks says you can join the crew's mess because of your work. Then this evening stay with me and we'll make the rounds of the promenade deck. The ladies will be out in fine fashion taking in the evening air. The men will be playing cards or dominoes, so the ladies have no one to talk with. Sometimes they talk with me, asking about the town or the river and such, sometimes just talking 'till the twilight fades. Once in a while they will hire me for a chore. What say you?"

Lyss replied with a grin, "Better yet!"

True to form, the morning began with a spectacular sunrise breaking over the Kentucky hills. Lyss tossed wood and coal eagerly, though with growing concern about his clothes. Tevia kept him entertained with river stories. Tevia also informed him that the *Clarion* would bypass Kentucky ports short of Louisville.

Tevia pronounced, "Cap'n says that no Yankee worth his salt would favor any Kentucky wharf below Covington. Don't know what his itch is, but I've seen him snub good cargo for no apparent reason."

Ulysses speculated on the reason. He was reminded of his father often telling that as a youth Jesse had apprenticed in his brother's tannery in Maysville, Kentucky. He would always end the story, "As soon as I could, I left Kentucky and left the curse of slavery behind." Perhaps this was the Captain's thinking, or perhaps it was a bad business deal that soured him on the region. Ulysses chided himself for letting his father's stories interrupt his steamboating adventure.

Tevia continued, "When we get to Vevay, and we always stop at Vevay, keep an eye on the Cap'n. He'll tie up longer than necessary – longer than business would dictate. He'll make an announcement to the passengers that there will be an unusual delay for some reason or another. Then he'll stroll up the hill to the town market and make a show of examining all the wines available. You know, don't you boy, that Vevay makes the best wine on the continent. Well, he'll decide on a variety, the same one he always decides upon, and order three bottles. Now you watch when he settles up; no cash is to be seen. The fix is in. Now don't you go tellin' this, boy, but I figure there must be an arrangement with the town to get all the passengers up to the market. That's what I think! Now that's just for you and me, right? Yeah, we'll ship a few cases downstream or upstream and take a box on for the boat. But that's not the real reason for the stop, and a long stop at that."

Lyss thoughtfully replied, "Well, I guess every business has its tricks of the trade. Captain Hendricks seems to have mastered his. He has a lot of responsibility. Not only for piloting the boat, and for the passengers and cargo, but to make a profit. Without a profit there's no boat to pilot. People see a steamboat captain and think of him only as a pilot. Pa always says, 'A business without a profit is not a business.'"

Tevia retorted, "Ha! Let me guess your father's motto: Work for work's sake."

"No," Lyss corrected, "but he does say, 'The only place success comes before work is in a dictionary'!"

Tevia slapped his knee, "Now I know where you get your stuff, boy! You know, I used to work just for money. But money always came up short. It seemed that I was just chasing after the wind. Now, here where I am, I work a little then I watch the river a little. I work a little then I watch another steamer goin' opposite, or watch us overtake some flatboat. Tied up beside another boat at a wharf we exchange stories, some true, some not. Off days I pop a cork in the water and see what I catch. I work a little, I meet people, I see the towns, learn the trade goods. I get my meals, get a bed, get all this glorious scenery. I see more in a day than most see in a year. Sometimes we lay over three or four days and I have me a good time. All this and a little cash too, now ain't that fine?"

Ulysses had to agree that that was fine.

Madison Downbound

Hazy morning fog obscured the opposite bank from the Madison wharf. From the Indiana shore, the river, the sky, the trees across the way were only ghostly shadows in a white veil. Rumbling thunder indicated the night's thunderstorms were surely departing. A delay in departure could put the *Clarion* at her destination near dusk. Yet, misty waters were dangerous waters.

Captain Hendricks wagered on a quick clearing. "Fire her up!" he shouted as he rang the signals. He had ordered the boat to be loaded the previous evening. Barrels of lard, bacon, and salt pork filled every nook and cranny. This run downstream could show record profits. It would be a long day's travel to reach Louisville. Business as well as pleasure was luring him on to the city. But, the Captain understood that only safe passage would prove profitable.

Captain Hendricks told his first mate, "Hold the lines taut. We have a good half hour before the fog lifts. I'm going up the hill for pie and coffee. Don't take on any more passengers or freight."

Ulysses was slinging wood. As he stood to wipe his brow he witnessed the Captain leaving the boat.

Tevia saw a look of surprise on the boy's face, "Not to worry. The Cap'n sometimes leaves like that to stem the temptation to get under way. He's figured the sky and he'll be back just at the proper time for sailing, you can bet on that."

Lyss replied, "I'll trust his judgment."

Tevia, "Judgment, now that's a word for the Cap'n. He has more judgment than any judge I ever heard of. But, I gotta' wonder at all the load he's taken on. There's hardly room to work here. I can't understand how Madison can put out as much pork as Cincinnati. Cincinnati even has this canal that comes down from way up in the countryside – I've seen it."

Lyss, "Well, Madison has a road that reaches all the way to Indianapolis and from there on north. I haven't seen it, but Michigan Road is on all the maps. It's supposed to reach up to Lake Michigan. You can bet that there's plenty of corn fields along the way. It's easier to move hogs than corn, and easier to move lard than live hogs."

Tevia, "I always heard the easiest way to move corn is in whiskey barrels."

Lyss, "Yes, but you have to grind the corn to make whiskey. Then fuel a fire to heat it. Someone has to watch it day and night. It doesn't always turn out like you intend it to. And the government takes a tax on each and every drop."

Tevia, "You sure you aren't a banker's son or maybe a politician. You seem to know more than your share of the ins and outs of business."

Lyss, "That comes from taking my Pa to debating meetings. You can't help but hear more than you care to."

There he was again, bringing his Pa into adventure away from home.

Tevia shared, "Well, whatever it is, Madison has outstripped the other towns along here. If I ever decide to settle down, I think that Madison may be the place to do it. Now, don't get me wrong, I said 'if.'"

Lyss, "You may have something there. All the towns I've seen down this river are cleaner and more industrious than Georgetown. My Pa bet on Georgetown when it became a new county seat. He's done alright by it. His business has prospered. He's bought and sold some town lots and some wooded land. It has been good to our family, for sure. The one thing that Pa never figured on though – today Southern sympathizers outnumber the Yankees in Georgetown."

Tevia snorted, "Now don't get me started on Copperheads! It'll ruin my entire day."

The pop-off valve hissed. Ulysses took off his gloves and leather apron. He looked around for a place to sit.

Patrick swung in over some barrels, "Lyss, you watch out for that guy in the brown suit!"

Lyss, "Do you mean the fellow that boarded at Lawrenceburg that looks down on his luck?"

Patrick, "Funny you should put it that way. I figure

him for a gambler and a conniver. He claims to be a friend of the gentleman farmer who boarded with him. But the other man took a stateroom and this guy is general passage. I figure he left Cincinnati out the back door and skedaddled to the next stop downstream."

Lyss, "He introduced himself to me, that's all. He called himself Emile LeMunyon. I did notice that he introduced himself to everyone. Sometimes he added 'Colonel' or 'Count' in front."

Patrick, "In Madison I noticed him eyeing you. I'd be careful. He'll take your money or your goods with dice or cards. If not, he'll find another way. Like I said earlier, the river brings out the best in some and the worst in others. He's one of the 'others.'"

Lyss shrugged off the suggestion, "Well, I've no money to speak of and my goods are stored in the middle of the boat."

Patrick answered, "You've been warned! And Cap'n Hendricks told him to quit fraternizing with the stateroom passengers. He's restricted him to the boiler deck."

"Cap'n aboard!" Tevia shouted.

Patrick headed for his station. Ulysses took up a new position near the paddlewheel. Off they went on the last leg of the downriver journey. According to Patrick it would be fifty miles of river with only a quick fuel stop. The sound of the thrashing paddles soon transfixed him. Both shorelines gradually emerged from the fog becoming once again beautiful unbroken green ribbons of forested hills. Ulysses laid aside his drawing pad and pencil; he laid aside his plans to select a scene to sketch.

Ulysses tried to imagine the vast extent of the Ohio River. Even the short section that he had witnessed seemed too grand to comprehend. His exhilaration changed the Ohio into a river of dreams – dreams of a carefree life. A big country it is, this America. One day he planned to see the entire river, all the rivers, then select choice acreage on a bluff for a farm of his own. He could raise horses of a premium nature. He would have an orchard overlooking a wide bend. He would have his own wharf to transport horses and to receive buyers who came from afar to select a prized animal. He began to lay out farm buildings and calculate acreage.

Left bend, right bend, one after another they were rounded. Each was different in its own way. The rising heat of the summer day made it difficult to stay on task. The rhythm of the paddlewheel and swaying course of the vast boat finally overcame his ability to fight off slumber's veil.

He jerked awake unaware that he had been asleep. The penetrating rays of the sun said differently. Somehow it had reached high up in the sky. Beside him the paddlewheel kept its regular thumping of the water. Hunger drove him to his feet. He scurried to the top of the freight pile to find what was left of his food cache. The middle of the boat was quickly heating. He did not dally, but promptly headed forward to catch a breeze. Bright sun bouncing off the water's placid surface blinded him. He began feeling his way amongst the bales and barrels while holding his lunch in a bandanna.

"Careful, boy!" A passenger in leather pants leaned back out of Lyss' way, "One bad step and you'll be overboard!"

"Pardon me, sir," Lyss shielded his eyes, "I will be careful, thank you."

A few more steps and he plowed into a man heading aft. "Pardon me, sir, the sun got me."

"Never you mind, Laddie," the man bowed, "step right on as you please." He put his right hand on Ulysses' left shoulder, "Wait, wait, now I have it! I knew I had seen you at some assembly. Yes, yes, your name is Hurcules, no Hermes – Hermes, am I correct?"

Lyss, "My Christian name is Hiram, but I am known by my middle name, Ulysses."

"Ah, Ulysses, yes. You were with Senator Hamer. It was at a courthouse in Batavia, north and east of Cincinnati as I recollect. I was the opposition in a debate with the Senator. You drove him, him and two others. The one spoke, a very stubborn man, not very sporting about the topic if I recall. A cattle buyer he was, and the other man a blacksmith from Bethel I believe. Well dressed they were for townsfolk; well read I declare. I believe I introduced myself earlier on this little voyage, Colonel LeMunyon at your service. Tell me, is my recollection correct?"

"Yes, sir, I drove to Batavia many times. It would have been Congressman Tom Hamer. He is the representative from Georgetown, not senator. The blacksmith from Bethel is my Uncle Samuel Simpson. The other man is my father Jesse Grant of Georgetown.

He is a businessman and runs a tannery. He delves into politics on occasion – was previously mayor and head of the Masons."

Emile patted the boy on the back, "I must say, Laddie Grant, you look the part of a businessman yourself. That's what I noticed about you back in that Ohio town, how businesslike you were for a youngster. Esquire Grant places a great deal of confidence in your business skills, I should say, sending you off by yourself with such important matters, and so many scoundrels about. But, I am sure that you were given ample instruction. Be vigilant, Young Ulysses, that is my advice. Keep a wide berth of the riffraff. If you need a friend, you can turn to me. A friend of the honorable Mr. Hamer is a friend of mine, shake on it!" Emile extended his hand which Ulysses shook. "I would offer you a cigar if you were not such a cub. You don't smoke cigars at home do you?"

Lyss quietly replied, "No sir."

Emile waved a new cigar and gave a sharp laugh, "Well Laddie, you're out on your own now, so I guess it's your choice." Looking at Ulysses' meager bandanna he bragged, "If I had known, I could have brought you something from the dining room. I could go back up, but I promised a gentleman to discuss business, you understand. You go on and enjoy what you have now, and don't forget if you need advice, I'm your man! Go on now, Young Ulysses, I shall look you up later after I complete my business."

Ulysses briefly considered making a statement in

defense of the food supplied by his mother and Mrs. Bailey but quickly realized there was no need. He knew from Patrick that Colonel LeMunyon was barred from upstairs to eat or for any other reason. Ulysses could have told how he has the privilege of supping with the crew. But that would be a boast, and one thing Ma would never stand for was a braggart. "The Lord shall cut off all flattering lips and the tongue that speaketh proud things," she would quote from Psalms. And follow from Proverbs, "When pride cometh, then cometh shame, but with the lowly is wisdom." He held his tongue.

Ulysses bowed and softly spoke, "Good day, sir, and pardon my clumsiness."

He wiped his forehead with his sleeve and again sought a cooler spot for his repast. He found all the choice locations occupied. He looked about for a way to maneuver. While jostling to the right he stumbled on a coil of rope. Regaining himself, he heard a sweet voice calling from above.

"Boy, oh boy! Up here! Yes, you young man, look at me!" He saw a wide white straw hat with a purple ostrich feather leaning over the railing. "Come up here, please. Come on, it will be alright, I will take responsibility. That's right, I'll meet you right here!"

Ulysses hesitated briefly, then thought, "Well, the next deck up would certainly be less crowded and undoubtedly cooler."

Up the grand staircase he went, somewhat timidly, somewhat enthusiastically. At the top of the stairs he halted. He spied two young ladies gaping at him. The one on the left, the one who had called, was tall and lean with flowing golden hair. The other was shorter, stouter, with brown hair tied back. Both wore floor length long-sleeved dresses; the first's all white, the second's yellow with blue trim and a yellow hat that hung low all around her head like a weeping willow tree.

"See, Ida," the first cooed, "it's that darling boy that I was telling you about."

Ida smiled. "Lovely," she said.

Ulysses was unnerved.

"Well, come over young man," the first ordered, "don't just stand there. You're likely to take a tumble down the stairs. Now, come hither. What's your name, boy?"

Lyss swallowed, then mumbled, "Ulysses, ma'am."

"What say you? Ulysses? That's no name for a precious boy. Just look at you, blue eyes, rosy cheeks, and sandy hair!"

Ida chimed in, "I do declare, Ellie, a perfect doll face, if ever I saw one!"

Ulysses cringed. Did she have to say "doll face" the same as did the teasing Georgetown girls.

Ellie winked, "And look, his cheeks are getting even rosier as we speak!"

Ulysses felt like his knees were going to give way.

Ellie commanded more sternly, "Come help us, please. Ida wishes to have this canopy extended. The cords are tangled, the mechanism is stuck, it just won't work, and there isn't a soul to help us. You look as if you possess the faculty to master it."

Ulysses gained courage and stepped forward. He placed his bandanna on a stand, "It is my pleasure to assist, if I can."

Ida commented, "Oh dear! We have interrupted Ulysses' lunch. And look, he's perspiring from the sun. Please, Ulysses, sit and eat. The task can wait a tad."

Ulysses assessed the problem with the canopy and was emboldened by knowing that he could handily dispense with it. "Thank you ma'am, but no," he said. "It should take only a moment to create a spot of shade, if all goes well. I'll be done and gone and you may resume your activity. You may call me Lyss, that's what I go by."

Ida pleaded, "You must stay and have your meal. It's the least we could do for you, to share our shade. It must be beastly hot down near the engine. Look, there's no breeze down there, and so crowded."

Ellie, "We have nothing to do for the day – just passing the time watching the river. Your presence will be no hindrance. Ida and I have been conversing ever since Washington City and have until Memphis. Not to offend, Ida, but our conversations have become as thin as a butterfly's wing. Stay and tell us about the Ohio country. I saw you come aboard at that hamlet above Cincinnati. What do you people do in Ohio?"

Ulysses was trapped. Panic fluttered. It gradually subsided as he loosened the cords and straightened the reeds. Working with his hands always calmed him. A day spent plowing a field, raking hay, or shucking corn may put kinks in his muscles, but it would undo kinks in his brain. When working a new horse, his world shrank until only the horse itself existed. Each flash of its eye, each twitch of its muscle, each placement of its hoof was dramatic in his concentration as though a volcano was creating new earth. With the horse released, Ulysses' concentration broken, calmness always enveloped him. He tried to apply these thoughts to his newfound situation.

Ida chided her friend, "Ellie, you invited him here. Now go find some sweet tea for Lyss. We must entertain him properly. Tea for all of us and some cheese and wafers. Now off with you! Meantime I'll instruct him on your impetuousness."

Ellie scolded, "Don't you dare! You behave now; I'll be right back."

Ida spoke soothingly, "Ellie is such a tease. I apologize for joining in her charade. Thank you for your willingness to help, and you certainly are mechanically inclined. Do sit a spell and enjoy our shade, some cool air, and Ellie will return with some refreshments, that is, unless she can charm some man to take care of it."

Ulysses reluctantly took a chair, but soon felt comfortable conversing with Ida.

Ida asked, "How does it happen that such a well-dressed young man such as you is traveling alone on a steamboat? Are you to visit relatives?"

Ulysses responded, "Yes and no. You see, I am headed to Louisville to visit a relative, a distant relation that I have never met. He has set up a new general store there at Third and Chestnut. I've seen a map; it should be easy to locate. Fifth Street runs straight up from the public landing all the way to Chestnut. I will pass five churches along the way. When I get to the Catholic church I will need to be on the alert for his shop. There is a public school also, three stories, that will be easy to find. He is to distribute some of my father's wares to other businesses. I am also to return with a legal deposition from him concerning some ancient family property in Connecticut. My father is delving into our family history and came upon some documents."

He realized that he was going against all advice by divulging his dealings. However he continued, "I'm inspecting each port of call and intend to walk each and every street in Louisville."

Ida gushed, "How enterprising of you. And what have you witnessed on these inspections?"

He shared his wanderings and his impressions. She listened attentively. They realigned their chairs first left then right to keep the shade as the boat rounded a horseshoe bend.

"I would be interested in your opinion of Memphis," Ida shared, "You must visit our city one day."

Ellie glided up, took a chair, and fanned herself.

"Ellie," Ida scolded, "We promised our helper some tea!"

"It is on its way, my dear," Ellie flipped.

Emile LeMunyon appeared carrying a tray, "Here we are, ladies, let me pour for you. Why, Young Ulysses! It is my honor to meet you again." He filled the glasses. "I was just thinking, I will arrange with an associate of mine in Louisville to provide a drayman to advance our young friend's freight from our boat to its destination. I will lay over and see that everything is expedited satisfactorily. I will provide trustworthy personnel to alleviate you from any concerns about dealing with strangers – you cannot trust just everyone, you know. A friend of Congressman Hamer deserves the most acute attention for his safety. I beg your pardon, ladies, for talking business. Let us enjoy this voyage. The Ohio is the most scenic of all the rivers, is it not?"

Ellie chided, "The scenery is beautiful, constantly beautiful, constantly for the past week. A little business talk is welcomed by me. I am not an empty headed belle. I have been known to conduct some business for myself. Now, what were you telling those gentlemen about land opportunities in Arkansas, something about a new western shipping port for cotton?"

Emile bowed to Ida, "I believe I introduced myself yesterday. Miss Ida, is it not? I beg a thousand pardons for interrupting your visit with the lad. I shall return another time. I shall just finish my tea and be on my way."

Ida, "A pleasure, visit us at your pleasure."

Ellie boldly stated, "Not so fast, Colonel. I asked about your investment proposal. You sit right here until I have heard your say. I am as capable as any of those men of assessing the possibilities."

Ida, "Ellie, please! I am sure the Colonel meant no insult. Certainly he has other things requiring his attention."

Emile set down his unfinished glass, "Heaven

forbid! I meant no judgment. I now understand that you desire to momentarily forgo the amenities of this voyage to inform yourself of an alluring proposition that could be of great benefit to your well-being."

Ida rolled her eyes. She glanced to Ulysses with a look of disappointment. Ellie grabbed the bodacious gentleman's right cuff and pulled him into a seat. Her eyes were wide with anticipation. Ulysses refilled his glass and drank it down. He prayed that Ida would not reveal details about his mission. He judged that she would keep their conversation confidential. There seemed to be a natural trust between them.

Emile leaned close and softly warned, "This is not for the public. You must not tell anyone what I am about to share. Only a select few shall be in the vanguard of this development."

Ulysses stood and coughed, "I must be excused. Thank you for the refreshments. Thank you for your company; I trust that you will enjoy the remainder of your voyage."

Ida reached out her hand for him to take, "You have been both kind and helpful. Please stop back before you debark."

Ellie, "Yes, thank you for your kindnesses. Now, Colonel, carry on, I too know some things about cotton."

Ulysses searched the boat until he found Patrick. Patrick absorbed the developments and headed directly to the pilothouse. It was only a short time until Patrick returned and yanked Ulysses up the staircase and around to a secluded spot where they could witness upcoming events. Ulysses was uneasy, sure that something was about to happen, but unsure about what it would be and what his degree of involvement might be.

Tevia, accompanied by two roustabouts, came scurrying up the staircase. Captain Hendricks descended a ladder, straightened his coat and cap, and briskly stepped forward. Tevia and his companions fell in behind. Together they marched in formation to the table that Ulysses had recently left.

Captain Hendricks barked, "Mister LeMunyon, you had your warning! You will now leave my boat!"

Emile took a sip of tea, "Yes, Captain, I have plans to debark at the next stop. I have business to attend in Louisville."

Captain Hendricks ordered, "Enough of your gobbledygook! Now! You will leave now!"

Emile questioned, "What do you intend? Right in the middle of the stream?"

Captain Hendricks, "You have your choice. I will put in to the Indiana bank and drop you off, or, if you refuse, yes, right here in the middle of the stream!"

Emile knew the Captain had complete authority and the means to carry out his order. It would be useless to spurn him. There would be no way to cajole him from his demand. Emile resigned to maritime justice. "Please excuse me ladies, the Captain requests my presence."

The Captain chose the tail end of a cut-bank to make a touch landing. Tevia escorted Emile to the tip of the extended gangway. Patrick shuffled behind with the dreg's leather bag. He deftly gave it a toss, landing it perfectly half on the shoreline and half just short.

Tevia proclaimed, "Don't cha' come back drummin' your bamboozle aboard the *Clarion* if ya value your life! I'll skin ya with a dull knife and nail your hide to a tree!" He pointed to a bare spot between trees. "Jump quickly now," Tevia laughed, "if you hope to find terra firma!"

Louisville

Passengers grumbled as Captain Hendricks pulled up to a nameless pier on the Indiana side. What had been a long steamy day was now growing short. All were anxious to reach Louisville. For some it was their destination. For most the town's hotels and restaurants would be a respite before continuing their journey. The Captain was just as eager as anyone to arrive before nightfall. Economy, though, dictated that he stock up here where boiler wood was cheap. He would load just enough wood to get to port and return to this ramshackle dock. Impatience grew as laborers moved slowly in the summer's heat.

The task completed, a quick blast of the whistle and they were again on their way. The short stint to the Louisville waterfront passed quickly. All on board shuffled to the front to gaze ahead. They ignored the Indiana towns of Jeffersonville and Clarksville in favor of the city with a more familiar name. Their vessel skimmed near Preston's Wharf and on down past the ferry dock to

the Public Landing. Here the *Clarion* moored just above
the inlet to the Louisville and Portland Canal.

The grand canal, a full fifty feet wide, had opened
for steamboat traffic only five years ago. It bypassed the
Falls of the Ohio, a run of heavy rapids that tumbled for
more than a mile through several finger-channels
between islands. The river dropped a total of thirty feet
over its course. Prior to the canal only flatboats or
keelboats with daredevil pilots, during particular stages
of river flow, dared chance passage. Previously most
vessels had to be unloaded, goods portaged, boats
laboriously lowered, and reloaded at great expense plus
loss of time. Louisville owed its existence to this only
obstacle to river traffic between Pittsburgh and New
Orleans. With the onset of steamboats, obviously too
large and unwieldy to portage, moving not only
downriver but up, the falls partitioned the river into two
distinct sections. The necessity of a bypass canal was
obvious.

Clarksville and Indiana had vied with Louisville and
Kentucky as to which side of the river would host the
proposed canal. Schemes came and went, politics to the
fore. Surprisingly, President Jackson vetoed a bill that
would have favored his Kentuckian constituency. Finally,
necessity reigned supreme. Curiously, the prime
financial support for the canal came from Pittsburgh
merchants who expected to be the beneficiaries of
unencumbered steamboat transport from their city
through to the West.

The *Clarion* was adeptly secured. Wayfarers on the

boiler deck bided their time while the excited stateroom passengers were escorted down the grand staircase. Yeomen trailed with trunks and bags and miscellaneous paraphernalia down the gangway and up the landing to waiting carriages and mule carts. On shore, hawkers offered every kind of service. Sellers brandished merchandise from flowers to parasols to peanuts.

Ulysses went to the stern to catch a view of the falls. All he could make out was rippling water and lines of trees. He looked for the canal gates. Again only water and trees. Disappointed, he went amidship to stand guard over his leather goods amid the frantic unloading activity. Passengers who had been serene while on the river suddenly became restless, if not agitated, shouting for special attentions of the purser and the roustabouts. Each demanded that his personal urgency be addressed. The stevedores took it all in stride. They maintained a measured rhythm in their chore. They instinctively understood that there was a natural sequence of clearing the boat of its cargo. To place the wants of any particular individual out of the normal order would break the rhythm, slow the entire process, and may even insert danger.

A sidewheeler suddenly appeared from the head of the canal. Its sideboard identified it as the *Pearl* out of Natchez. The boat quickly slipped in adjacent to the *Clarion*. Soon the unloading frenzy doubled. Ulysses understood that his packs would be "last off." He kept his place while studying the workers. Each worked with minimal direction, understanding his own skills and responsibilities and also those of his co-workers. Like a procession of ants in a summer's orchard they efficiently conducted their task. The crew of the *Pearl* respected the implied space on the landing claimed by the *Clarion* as if the two crews were one. As the boat was cleared, the orderly stash on the landing marched down closer to the waterline.

Ulysses' turn finally came. He picked up his own rucksack and one of the smaller bundles and followed four stevedores who hauled the rest. All was stacked next to the common freight heap where two crewmen stood watch. Lyss climbed atop his pile and waited for the commotion to die down. This landing certainly was more congested than Cincinnati's – and more chaotic. Perhaps his unfamiliarity exaggerated the chaos. Slowly but surely draymen began hauling away freight – some to their final destinations, some to points of transfer. Patrick remained active assisting the purser. The boat maintained responsibility for each item of common freight until it was claimed from the manifest.

Tevia brought Ulysses a tin of cool water, "Your relative gonna' show?"

Lyss shrugged, "I'll wait for awhile to see if he comes by. He has no way of knowing on which boat or when I'm to arrive. I'll have to wait and see."

Tevia suggested, "When the hubbub settles, me and Patrick we'll formulate a plan." Off he went.

Ulysses studied the variety of steamboats lining Louisville's waterfront: large; small; elaborate; mundane; floating palaces; workaday tenders. Most, like the *Clarion,* were somewhere in between – built not only to accommodate both freight and passengers at city docks, but made of shallow draft and wide beam in order to nudge up to shore at any chosen spot. If night or weather or river conditions dictate they could pull in and tie up to trees, "choke a stump" in river vernacular, until the way is clear.

Decrepit warehouses and shabby saloons were all that Ulysses could see from his perch. He watched roustabouts wrestle some mechanical contraption from the *Pearl's* deck. It was made with a heavy wooden frame held together by long bolts. The machine had gears and sprockets here and there, but nothing to indicate its purpose.

From the *Pearl* emerged a group of Army officers. Whence had they come: New Orleans; Natchez; Vicksburg; Memphis? Perhaps from some post on the western frontier up the Red River? Whither were they bound? Was this their destination? Or Philadelphia, Washington City? What had they given up to don the uniform of their country? Had they fought in the Seminole War or skirmished with tribes on the western frontier?

Patrick tossed Lyss a bag of peanuts, "Here, catch! I brung ya somethin' else – got it right here in my pocket! A present! You'll never guess!"

Lyss never liked to guess. He shrugged as he shelled a peanut.

Patrick continued, "Here in my pocket is somethin' I've never had in my possession before – and it's just for you!" He gave an exaggerated laugh along with a little dance. Tevia came up while his buddy proceeded with his fun. "Now let's see, Miss Ida never said good-bye to you, did she, nor did her skinny friend?" He peered close to Lyss' face to see the desired reaction. "Ya know, I don't think her friend appreciated you poking your nose into her business. But Ida sure did! Yes, she did fer certain! She gave me two bits jest to have me bring you this!"

Patrick pulled out a frilly handkerchief and waved it back and forth. He held it over his head and danced a jig. Ulysses could not conceal his blushing. His throat began to swell.

Tevia caught the meaning, "Oh, so you're her knight in shining armor! Her gladiator! Lord have mercy!"

Patrick jeered, "I got hard cash and you got this!"

Patrick flipped the delicate lacy cloth to Lyss. They waited for Lyss' response. He had none. He was frozen in place. Two of the three had a good laugh.

Finally, Patrick moved to other matters, "Cap'n has given leave to some of the crew – says you can have a berth while we are in port. He wants to thank you for the LeMunyon matter and says you can have free passage up to your home port. He'll have handbills printed in the morning advertisin' departure for Marietta in three days. I'd say check in each day jist to be sure. Now, what about your wares?"

Lyss was relieved to be centered on business. He quickly tucked the gift into his waistband. "I'm expected to stay with a distant cousin who moved out here from

Charleston, Virginia. He's setting up a mercantile. I need to get word to him that I've arrived, but I don't want to leave my father's merchandise."

Tevia motioned towards the two crewmen overseeing the remaining freight, "These boys will keep an eagle eye out. You jist go ahead."

Lyss, "I'd rather not."

Patrick offered, "Tevia and me, we know parts of the town. We intend to go gallivanting about, carouse a bit anyway. Give us the name and place and we will give him notice. What say?"

Tevia nodded confirmation.

Lyss, "Fine. I have never met him. His name is Noah Tompkins. His place of business is at Third and Chestnut. Directions are to go straight up Fifth Street – you know where that is?"

Tevia pointed straight in front of them, "Right there."

Lyss, "Good! Go up past the Catholic Church."

Tevia, "Yeah, I know it, I do."

Lyss, "Go on past City School and you'll come to Chestnut. Make a left and over to Third, then inquire – less than a mile total I'm told."

Tevia, "Easy enough. Leave it in our hands. You'd better write a note of introduction so's he'll know to trust us two vagabonds."

The two boatmen quickly dispensed with their promised task. Tompkins agreed to hire a drayman right away "even though it will cost extra so late in the day." By nightfall the load and the boy were appropriately delivered to their final destination.

Ulysses discovered Noah Tompkins living in a stark room above his wood framed store. The man hoped to bring his family from Charleston by early autumn. The first room down the hall was a makeshift woodshop where Noah had in process the making of store shelving. This room also contained Ulysses' bed – a suitably converted crate with straw mattress.

A hired slave brought in supper of soup with bread and milk. Noah set up a temporary table where they ate as they went over the business at hand. First was to unpack and check the leather inventory. Next Lyss presented the envelope he had carried for his father.

Noah assured, "Looks good to me. I will need to add one line. I can have this deposition witnessed and stamped tomorrow afternoon. I will send it and one additional document back with you. If your father Jesse is successful with this old family claim back in Connecticut, well the whole clan will celebrate."

His father also had sent a list of items for Lyss to locate and jot down prices. He had explained to his son, "Though I sell such and such for a particular amount at home, it may be worth more or less at Cincinnati depending on the number of suppliers and the market. Up at Marietta or down at Madison conditions may be different and the price set accordingly. The same goes for buying supplies. So it pays to know the market values where you intend to participate. If it's not a paying proposition, then it's time to look elsewhere."

Noah began drawing a crude map and marked

locations where Lyss could check items off his list. He added a warning, "Stay between Second and Seventh and you should be safe." He went on telling about his aspirations for his new store, "Not just retail, but to supply smaller places on the interior." While cigar smoke curled around his head, he used phrases like: "The sweetest plum is always highest upon the tree;" and "Strive to attain the highest good for fellowman;" and "I've learned to trust a man who feeds himself after his stalls are all fed." Of his trust in his hired slave Benjamin he offered, "The man's clothes don't fit him, but he fits me fine." Ulysses had no doubt that his father and Noah were related.

Noah queried, though somewhat rhetorically, "What is the word on banks in Ohio? Every week I get a New York newspaper and every week another bank has failed. Banks around here are tightening up on loans. They're squeezing the little guys and start-ups like me while they favor the big outfits. Nothing fair about it! I'm good for a while, but if my prospective clients can't get loans they can't buy. I've got to keep merchandise moving to make a go of it."

Noah went on a tirade against President Andrew Jackson and the newly installed President Van Buren. "Before long paper won't be any good and we'll have to deal in hard silver or gold. If it all caves in, I think I will fold and take off for Michigan. In a brand new state there should be brand new opportunities. I admit though, I don't know a thing about Michigan. Another plan is to procure a government contract to supply hardware and harness for the removal of the Cherokee Nation. I am actively looking into that – government specie ought to remain solid enough. Some of the Cherokee are already being rounded up. It's been a long and drawn-out process, but in my mind it's likely to happen soon. Imagine how many wagons it will take to move so many people clear out to Indian Territory beyond Arkansas. Each wagon means a team of horses. Each team means a set of harness. Every four wagons mean a kitchen. Add to that spare parts, if you will. Not that I concur with the country's stand on the issue, mind you. The census showed over fifteen thousand souls. Being a government process, I figure it will take four years, maybe five.

"It has been well over a year since Texas got her independence. Within five years she will most likely join the states on an equal footing. Imagine the number of people hereabouts who will want to settle in that wide-open land once it is an actual state. Now, somebody has to outfit those settlers, don't they? Flatboats will appeal to some for the first leg, but families will feel safer in their familiar wagon. The first step in being a merchant is exploring opportunities and being ready when they turn fruitful."

Lyss kept a list of his own – a list of sites to see in Louisville. See the stately new Marine Hospital building, definitely out of bounds on the southeast side. See a steamboat pass through the canal locks, also out of bounds to the northwest. See the Galt House, only slightly out since it faced Second Street. Washington Hall was within limits as was the ferry, at least while the ferry was on this side of the river. As the lamp wick began to sputter, he was thinking about a fine breakfast at the Galt House.

In the morning Ulysses dodged Noah's propensity for talking about his business plans. Stepping out the front door Lyss turned east and caught the first rays of the sun. One block over and down Second Street towards the river he went. No shops and only a couple restaurants were open so early. He passed on towards the Galt House on Main. He would have two full days to explore the city. From what he could judge, Louisville appeared to be about half the size of Cincinnati. It had only a portion of the newer grand buildings that he knew there. Louisville still had shades of a frontier settlement. Rickety frame stores sat intermingled with old stone buildings and the occasional fine bank or trading center. Old buildings were everywhere being torn down to make way for new. He planned to investigate construction soon to be finished on the new Court House. Yet, townspeople seemed to cling to their backwoods heritage.

Ulysses crossed Market Street and was within a block of his destination. He peered at titles in a bookstore window. He walked directly into an iron rod being held across a man's chest. The man reeked of a variety of barnyard odors. A filthy felt hat flopped down to his eyebrows. Long stringy hair protruded below. Weathered skin was covered with scraggly whiskers which in turn were covered with tobacco stains.

Lyss balked at the man's smelly hot breath as he

bellowed, "Don't ya cross, boy! Take a step back! Pay attention now!"

Lyss did step back with a jerk. He saw another ruffian unlock an iron gate and swing it wide. "Alright now, step down, out with ya!" He looked upon a black man in soiled sackcloth stepping out to the sidewalk. The man was followed by another and another. Soon there was an entire procession. Single file they shuffled towards two waiting wagons. Faint letters on the sides of each wagon identified "Garrison Slave Trader."

Ulysses quickly realized he had quite literally stumbled upon the infamous slave pens that he had read about in abolitionist tracts. Each man in line braced iron chains on his wrists that wrapped around his waist. The men were strung in line on a heavy iron chain running through leg shackles. They hobbled along in unison. They deftly stepped up empty wooden crates into the wagons. Their empty faces looked down as if peering into a void. All except one. One large middle-aged man freely let tears roll down his face. His eyes were devoid of hope – only despair lingered.

The nearest of three guards wielding shotguns struck the weeping man's neck with his barrel, "Quit 'cher bawlin' you jackass. I've had enough of you!" Another guard whacked the man's back with an iron rod. Whack! Whack! Whack!

The man cried aloud, "Whar are ya, Mammy? I want ya here! Lord, send her along! Please, Lord, Please!"

Whack! Tears streamed. He blubbered openly. His companions nudged him along. Feet shuffled. Chains rattled. The man muttered incoherently. Whack!

Ulysses felt heavy in his stomach. His chest heaved. He beat a hasty retreat back around the corner. Over to First Street he went to make a detour from the scene. On First he saw other wagons with other names – other slave gangs, chains, shotguns, prods, despair.

He decided to forego breakfast.

Maysville

Young Ulysses took in the view from the crest of the hill he had just climbed. This was the spot from where he had always hoped to do a sketch of the town and landscape. Each opportunity had vanished as he yielded to errands of important degree. Again today duties were necessitating that he move along. The broad Ohio River flowed from the east where the sun was now making its day's appearance under dark tufted clouds, coloring them salmon with streaks of purple. The river bent in a smooth arc towards him then swept away to disappear several miles to the northwest. The hills across the way in the Buckeye State rose as high as the Kentucky hill on which he stood, some three hundred feet above the river.

Ten miles downriver lay the familiar town of Ripley. It had been three months since he had seen it or had been home to Georgetown. Immediately below him, nestled tightly against the river was Maysville, still called "Limestone Landing" or simply "Limestone" by old-timers and boatmen. The village spanned only three blocks back from the river before creeping up the lower reaches of the steep incline. Hanging from the hillside below him, newer homes fronted narrow lanes.

From somewhere far to the east, thunder reverberated down the river valley from the remains of a storm that shook Maysville during the night. Ulysses had welcomed the downpour and the cracks of lightning when they began to play. Booming thunder rattled windows throughout the night. It was the first thunderstorm of the season, heralding an end of a relentless winter. Here, high on the hill as the sky began to clear, he sniffed the air. He could smell the earth coming alive. He longed to see the green back in the trees. He longed to be back home plowing fresh fields behind a trusty team.

Ice flows created a patchwork of white against dark water. There was no river traffic this morning. One lonely steamboat was at the landing, and it had no steam up. Only the ferryboat showed signs of activity. Two deckhands astern were coiling rope. From here they appeared as mere spiders stringing a silky strand of web. A tow barge filled with coal and its companion empties lined the waterfront down from the landing. Grey smoke floated gracefully from dozens of chimneys.

He eyed Aunt Permelia's chimney. It was easy to distinguish among the short row of tall brick homes on Front Street, it being adjacent to the first coal barge. Ulysses had changed the night's coal fire over to apple wood. He knew that Monday was a day for baking. Aunt Permelia would surely welcome him with sweet rolls when he returned. She was the widow of his father's half-brother. His father Jesse had apprenticed in his youth in Uncle Peter's tannery, learning the trade before striking out on his own.

Uncle Peter Grant had expanded his tannery three times. He later bought into a coal mine plus a salt company on the Kanawha River up at Point Pleasant, Virginia. His company carried salt in its own barges to villages downriver. While supplying his own tannery, the company turned outstanding profits with its monopoly of the trade. One winter's day Uncle Peter, standing on the rail of a loaded barge, shoved his pike against another to put it in line. The pike slipped, Peter went into the frigid river and could not be rescued.

In addition to having five children in the household, Permelia has carried on the business interests to this day. She directs rental properties and she lets a room in her home to a boarder. Ulysses spied the window of the room that he is sharing with older cousin Solomon during his three-month school term. The window to the left hosts a boat engineer who has been absent during Ulysses' stay.

Ulysses instinctively looked to his right to gaze upon the tannery. The ever-present billows of dark smoke rose from the distinctive double stacks. Thankfully, he was only required to go there infrequently to carry papers to and from the office. Suddenly, a thought jumped into his mind. Why was it that the Grants seemed to prosper at a business that appeared to be only marginally successful for others? Every county has one or more tanneries –

each and every one a ramshackle affair, at least to his knowing. His Pa did speculate in vacant lots and also sold fire insurance for a company out of Columbus. His Pa and Aunt Permelia held status in their communities amongst the leading merchants, lived in strong brick houses, and dealt in public issues. Here he was, sent off to a notable school, "privileged" some would say. This idea he would have to give more thought some day.

A little to his left and directly below, built into the hillside near Lexington Pike, stood Maysville Academy. Ulysses always welcomed chances to experience surroundings in different towns. Yet, he had been apprehensive that he would not meet the expectations of the reputed academic institution. Instead he found the lessons tedious, simply repetitions of what had been covered at Georgetown's subscription school on Dutch Hill. The academy's Professor William Richeson was likeable enough and told interesting stories out of class, but was uninspiring during lectures. Lyss' term would end soon and he would be home well before his sixteenth birthday.

Ulysses had been to Maysville before on delivery trips. He recalled how he had on previous occasions taken loads up the Lexington Pike draw, passing nearby the academy without distinguishing it from other edifices. At the base of the hill oxen drovers had hawked their services to pull his wagon to the top, "You'll never make it with them horses, no siree. This drag takes an ox, maybe a team of four for what you've got." Ulysses, aware of the grade, always bid them ado and nursed his team to the top where he treated them each to an apple and an extra ration of oats. With his meticulous attention to the task at hand, he could not possibly be accountable for not noticing a building here or there.

Ulysses recalled how last fall he had feathered a carriage down the grade. John Payne, a Georgetown resident, booked passage to Flat Rock to look into a business opportunity offered by the man's brother. With little to do upon arrival, Ulysses had looked over the brother's horses. He offered a trade of one of his newly trained horses for a promising two-year old plus ten dollars. The offer was promptly accepted. The new horse had not been broken to harness and of course was not familiar to his trusty team lead, Prince. After lunch, on a road connecting to the Lexington-Maysville Pike, the horse was spooked by a mongrel dog and broke into a headlong run. Despite Ulysses' best efforts, the team and carriage careened side-to-side and off and onto the road. He finally got stopped not ten feet short of a menacing precipice at the junction. Payne immediately lunged off and held Prince's bit.

When the team was steadied, Payne exclaimed, "You take it from here how you wish. I'll see you in Georgetown! I advise you to dispose of this nag immediately! Look how she's shivering!" Payne grabbed his bag and hailed an approaching freight wagon, calling back, "Try not to destroy my merchandise."

Ulysses calmed the horses and led them on foot down the pike a ways. If he could just get to Maysville, he could borrow a horse and complete the trip as prescribed. Recalling an old trick he had heard, he removed his wide bandanna and covered the nervous young horse's eyes. From that moment the horse submitted to Ulysses' commands and Prince's lead. At the head of Maysville's Market Street, Payne had just dismounted from his rescue wagon as Ulysses pulled up. John Payne stood at the curb shaking his head in wonderment.

His current stay in Maysville excused Ulysses from his father's tirades on political issues. Yet here in the early morning on a hill above the town he could not escape. The Lexington Pike winding up below, the route he would be taking to the county seat at Washington, Kentucky was loaded with politics as much as it was with freight. It, along with the National Bank quagmire, was what had driven Jesse Grant away from the Andrew Jackson camp into the Whig Party. The state of Kentucky had finagled a bill in Congress to have the federal treasury pay half the cost of improving Limestone Trace to turnpike status. President Jackson vetoed the bill much to the outrage of his western supporters. Jesse Grant, once a Jackson delegate to the Ohio state convention, converted to the Whig party and never looked back. After a great deal of political upheaval, the state of Kentucky determinedly advanced the road project on its own accord.

A shaft of clear sunlight peered sharply between clouds onto the hilltop. Ulysses had delayed long enough. Before he left this charming venue, he glanced once again up and down the river just in case a paddlewheel steamer had rounded the distant bends. He had not encountered the *Clarion* since his return from Louisville. He longed to see Patrick, to see how he was faring. He thought about Tevia and the Captain. Perhaps another boat would bring the graceful figure of Ellie and the easy smile of Ida. On the other hand, LeMunyon may be skulking about with a long well-honed knife.

He would have to step quickly in a loop south and west to bypass a ravine and arrive at the toll house where he was to meet fellow classmate William Henry Wadsworth. He hoped he would chance upon a farm lane that would carry him there. He and Henry had met before sunrise on the covered porch of the academy. Ulysses was unable to convince his classmate to scramble through the brush up the steep hillside. Henry preferred to try his luck against the torrents that were washing through the ravine where there was supposed to be a road.

"Look at you, boy!" the toll man cried out, "You been wrestlin' a bear? Maybe a pair o' 'em the way you look. Come on in. The other boys are inside wringing out. I thought educated boys would know better than to be out and about on a mornin' like this one. Well, squeeze yourself inside."

Ulysses greeted his schoolmate and friend, "You know, Henry, it looks like we were both right. The hill was too slippery with ice and the road too swift with water."

Henry replied, "Or both wrong. I have to say, Toad, your aunt will be mortified at you being seen in

Washington the way you look. Better come back with some good ideas."

Lyss had picked up a new name in Maysville, "Toad", a name he couldn't shake.

The toll man, hoping to lure the boys into conversation opined, "Ideas are two a penny. It's action that counts!"

Not wishing to be delayed with small-talk, Lyss stated, "It's action for us! We'd better sally forth if we're to get there, do our business, and be back before nightfall."

With that the three boys sauntered along up the pike towards their destination. Boy number three was William Brewster. Henry invited him to tag along. Willie and Henry and Lyss were often teamed together for classroom debates. They generally did alright for themselves. Willie was a natural talker, though his voice was often more piercing than his arguments. Henry was good at digging up facts. Being of local stock he had a network of resources. Lyss appreciated the talents of both of the boys. Although Willie was occasionally irritating, Lyss appreciated his talent for talk the most. Lyss' stomach churned uncontrollably whenever he was pressed to talk in front of a group of any size. He would turn the occasion over to Willie whenever the situation allowed. Ulysses provided logic which he considered the key to winning debates. Everyone in the school recognized that he was the master of fitting arguments into an irrefutable sequence, omitting extraneous information that may detract from the conclusion, weaving a solid warp and weft.

Willie questioned, "What are we to do when we get to Washington? I chose 'Simon Kenton's Store,' but I don't know what I am to do with his store. I can't bring a store back now, can I? Where do I look for this store? I should have chosen Simon Kenton's comb. I could bring back a comb if I found it. Here I go sloshing up the pike with no inclination as to a purpose. If old man Richeson had told me, 'Go copy the cornerstone of the courthouse,' that I could do right off. How are we to debate a store?"

Henry tried to explain, "Our end is not a debate. It is merely to provide ammunition for a debate."

Willie quipped, "Well, if Simon Kenton left any ammunition in his store, I'll get some of it and plunk it down on Richeson's desk."

Lyss had a good laugh, "Henry, I have to say Willie got you on that one!"

Henry was not amused, "Well, I don't intend to walk all day and come back empty handed."

Lyss explained to the younger boy, "Willie, it's about what the professor calls 'research'. Each of us is to find a single fact, a tidbit if you will, that relates one way or another to the history of Madison County."

Willie, "Great! I'm done. It's a fact that Simon Kenton, the founder of Washington, Limestone Landing, and the county of Madison had a store in the town up yonder!"

Lyss continued, "The trick is that you need a tried and true document to justify what you just said."

Willie, "All right then, I shall write it down and

make it a fact."

Henry interjected, "That gobbledygook won't do! What you need is a court document, a survey map, a census, or an original newspaper article. To make points, a court document is best, maybe a lawsuit or criminal action. Even an old diary is good. In your case maybe an old bill of sale is the ticket."

Lyss chimed in, "Now remember, Professor Richeson has been doing this for years. He's heard just about every fact that one of us students is able to dig up. At least he thinks so. I figure that the more miniscule the item is, the higher the score. Find something that no student, or anyone else, has brought to light. That's my goal."

Henry instructed Willie, "You dug yourself into a hole when you chose Simon Kenton. He's the most famous guy there is hereabouts. Everything he ever touched has been raked over the coals time and again. You'll have to dig double deep to find something unique!"

Willie, "Ouch! If the professor asks again I'll volunteer for the top of the list of not signing up. I thought Toad was weird when he announced his topic."

Lyss divulged, "I recall Grandma Simpson claiming that William Wells came down the Ohio River from Pennsylvania as a five-year-old. His father was Samuel Wells who had a land grant because of his service in the Virginia Militia. She said he settled on a claim here before heading on to the environs of Louisville. Others say he went straight from Pennsylvania to Louisville. So, if I am able to find a deed with his name at the courthouse, I've got my Ace of Spades. That's my plan. Along with Kenton and Daniel Boone, William Wells would be the third famous frontiersman tied to the county."

Henry, "Excellent! And what if you don't find such a thing?"

Lyss, "I have a backup, sure enough."

Willie whined, "This is beginning to sound like real work. I've been to the courthouse in Lexington with my uncle. They have stacks and stacks of records. I'll still be flipping pages when I'm ninety-two and a half. One day some other student will come along and find me buried under a whole passel of ledgers. Hain't no way I'll scrounge up what you say I need."

Henry, "You don't go looking just willy-nilly. Clerks will direct where to start. I will help you phrase your inquiry. Sharpen your idea like you sharpen a pencil so that they can direct you proper."

Willie inquired, "Toad, what was that that you said about your backup? If you don't require it, perhaps it could be mine. No sense in throwing it away, now, is there? If it is an interesting fact, shouldn't it come out to the daylight?"

Lyss divulged, "Well, it goes back to a story I overheard at the newspaper office in Georgetown. My friend Dan Ammen's father is the editor. He was writing up an article about it: the post office at Washington was the first such establishment west of the Allegheny Mountains. That's it. I've never heard it mentioned around here. Either it is so much common knowledge or else no one knows about it."

Henry chided, "Now, Willie, that's Lyss' stuff 'till he gives it up. Don't go claiming it just yet."

The three trudged along through the mud called Lexington Pike. Their destination seemed to be getting farther rather than closer. Lyss' mention of his friend Dan made him feel even more isolated from his hometown. Dan was no longer there either. Dan, like Lyss, had been in a preparatory school of sorts. Jacob Ammen was Dan's older brother by fourteen years. Jacob had attended the Military Academy at West Point, New York. He graduated in 1831. After four years of regular service he returned to the academy as a mathematics instructor. Dan headed there a year ago to be tutored by Jacob in preparation for acceptance to Navy School. All proceeded according to plan. From there Dan, appointed by Congressman Thomas Hamer as a midshipman, went to the school in Philadelphia he had sought.

Dr. John Johnston drove his rig from a lane onto the pike ahead of the trio, "Ho, Lads! Climb on! No sense walking if you're headed to Washington town. One of you can drive while I nap. I've been up since two bells."

The boys wiped their boots as best they could and climbed aboard. Henry surprised Lyss by taking the reins. The good doctor told stories all the way to the courthouse. He never napped; Willie did. Doc Johnston couldn't say enough about his famous son: an industrious top-notch student; off to West Point; army service; the Blackhawk war; returning to Kentucky after resigning from the army; off to Texas; the fight for Texas independence; Brigadier General of the Texas Army; son Albert Sidney Johnston was now Secretary of War for the Republic of Texas. Illustrations jumbled one atop the other from the proud father.

Henry and Lyss took it all in, word for word.

Henry proclaimed, "We had a debate in January about Texas' decision to release Santa Anna. I thought of contacting you back then, but didn't. Now I know I should have done so. We won nevertheless."

Doc Johnston cleared his throat to begin another chapter.

Henry interrupted him, "Do you recall, some five years back, a young lady from Cincinnati came visiting Washington? Harriet Beecher, a woman teacher at the Western Female Institute. She has been writing articles in the Cincinnati papers, some of which have been picked up by other papers clear to Boston."

Doc replied demurely, "Yes, I recall. I've read some of her stuff, stirring up the abolition folks."

Henry grew excited, "You do? I'd like to know where she stayed, whom she dealt with, that sort of thing."

Doc, "Nobody paid much attention at the time. Sure, it was curious to have a female teacher about, advocating that women could do this and women could do that. She'd have women doctors, mind you. Harrumph! These days she has a hoopskirt posse agitating the entire Cincinnati community over a bunch of nonsense."

Henry, "So, you say you know whom she stayed with."

Doc, "She stayed at Marshall Key's. His wife hails from Cincinnati. They sent their daughter Liz to that female school. I tell you, as a doctor you bring all kinds of people into this world. Anyway, that Miss Beecher bedded there for a few nights. Of course, I knew at the time that her father Lyman had been riling against slave owners ever since he moved out here from Connecticut – writing tracts and all that. Lyman spouts off about the evils of Kentucky whiskey, none the less. Came west to save us from ourselves, did he? Next I suppose it will be our tobacco. If he doesn't like our ways, why didn't he stay put in the first place? I know what I'm talking about – I originated out of Connecticut myself. Some people are just natural agitators! If you happen to run across him, you just inform him that you know a doctor who will pay his fare back to New England or on to England itself if he desires!"

Henry thought to himself, "Some may have the same opinion of your son."

Doc continued, "Key's place is just down the pike from the courthouse, on the left. It's a well-kept brick home, easy to find. Ask anybody, they'll know it."

Henry replied, "Of course, the Marshall place. I know it. Sure, the Marshall place."

Henry confirmed his plan. His document would not be about ancient history. It would entail contemporary national issues landing in his home county.

The carriage remained quiet the remainder of the trip to Doc's house. Immediately south of the courthouse the horse instinctively turned up South Court Street. It halted at Doc's carriage house. The boys thanked their host.

"You boys want some breakfast?" Doc invited, "We'll whip something up shortly!"

Though tempted they all declined, "We'll have a meal later at Washington Hall. Thanks for the offer and thank you for saving our boots."

They scurried up a narrow path to the broad cobblestone sidewalk facing the stately courthouse. Thick walls of whitewashed native limestone rose two levels above the knoll. A massive stone tower poked higher through the middle of its roof. This in turn was heightened by a wooden tower which was topped by a cupola belfry which in turn was crowned with a stately copper weathervane. Between two large trees, stone slabs stepped up to a small portico facing huge double doors. On the tree to the north, official notices were posted on a board.

One in particular caught Ulysses' eye. "To be sold at public auction before the Courthouse door Washington, Kentucky – Negroes – by court order to settle the estate of James Beck of this county – Terms Cash – Samuel, age 59; Pauly, age 39; Ben, age 36; Lewis, age 34; Tomas, age 31; Eli, age 31; Charles, age 29; Liz, age 56; Mary, age 37; Maggie, age 33; Martha, age 30, Sally, age 15; 3 boys; 5 girls – Monday, March 26, 1838 – J.B. Archbold, Executor."

Lyss looked at his feet. On this very spot one week hence, men, women, and children listed on the bill would stand facing a crowd of onlookers: bidders; speculators;

curiosity seekers; families on outings; vagrants. He wondered if James Beck had been a responsible master.

"Do you know who James Beck was?" he asked Henry.

Henry shook his head, "Never heard of him. There's enough slaves listed here for a hemp farm. Maybe he ran a trade of some kind." Henry reflected, "Poor souls! In bygone years the whole slew of them most likely would have been sold as a lot and stayed in the neighborhood. But yesteryear is gone! With the demand for farm labor depressed in these parts most slaves don't even earn their keep. Thriving sugar and cotton fields way down the Mississippi are begging for more hands day in and day out. Likely some speculator flush with cash will jack up the price on the healthy males and the childbearing women. The speculators will have no personal interest in them, only to resell them to the slave pens in Lexington or Louisville who will then sell them at a premium on down the river. No doubt this lot will be broken up. It's a sad state of affairs. Old man Beck, whoever he was, would have been chided for selling off prime workers for a profit. But his heirs, well they're off the hook. The sale is to go through as a matter of course. Can they help it if their property is sold down the river? Some may shake their heads, but no one will find fault with this sale."

"Poor souls, indeed!" Lyss thought. His mind jumped back to his sojourn in Louisville. Thoughts that had lingered in his mind sprang to the forefront. Visions of his stroll down Second Street stole his senses. His mind filled with coffles of weary slaves, empty of aspirations, devoid of hope, bound to a chain wherever it was led. Those chains seemed to ring in his ears. A chill crept up his spine.

Willie piped up, "Hain't you seen a slave auction? I've been to lots of 'em in Lexington. Now tell me again what we are here for? Do they let you rip a page out of a ledger to use for your evidence? Does it have to be signed by Kenton himself? When's lunch?"

Willie stumbled on the first of three massive limestone slab steps. "Whoa!" He stooped and sat on the top step.

Henry scolded, "Quit stalling! In with you!"

Willie, "Give me just a minute. Toad, tell me, is that stone as big as the one you hauled into Georgetown?"

Ulysses pretended not to hear.

Henry asked, "What's this? Another Georgetown circus pony legend about that famous hometown Grant boy?"

"Tell him, Toad!" Willie encouraged, "I heard it from your cousin Solomon."

Henry, "Well, let's have it."

Lyss did not like hearing these stories and certainly did not care to tell them. Reluctantly he began, "People make it to be a bigger deal than it ever was. Doctor Buckner, new to town, had spied a naturally formed well-shaped rock on the edge of the bed of White Oak Creek. Many people in Georgetown have stoops at their front doors taken from the area. This one was better formed and larger than any collected."

Willie interjected, "Tell him how big it was. Huge, I

heard!"

Lyss continued, "Fact is it measured seven by four feet long and wide and five inches thick – certainly way bigger than anybody in Georgetown had. That's why Doc thought he needed it for his new house. Well, he contracted with Ralston's crew to bring it in. That gang of four lays foundations and retaining walls and such. They took their heavy wagon, four oxen, iron bars, jacks, chains and paraphernalia down to the creek and spent a day tussling against that rock. Their plan was to raise one end and slide the slab forward onto the wagon bed. I was at the creek fishing and watched the proceedings. They got one end raised a foot and four inches, well shy of the level of the wagon bed. From there one attempt after another with their levers proved fruitless at improving the position. Well before dusk they gave up and headed out. Back at town they broke the contract and went about other business."

The boys stepped aside to let two men enter the building.

Henry urged, "Go on, I'm listening."

Lyss gave a sly smile, "Over the week-end I found everything I needed in the tannery yard. A pair of oak timbers eight inches square, a length of machinery belting and rivets, heavy rope and some twenty-foot poles for levers and to make an A-frame."

Henry quickly interrupted, "A-frame?"

Lyss, "It's a savvy contraption woodchoppers use to heft cumbersome logs up out of a tight place. Anyway I removed the bed from my wagon and put the timbers down the length. With horsepower on the frame I managed to lift the back end of the stone. With levers and wedges I got it leveled even with the end already up."

Henry, "That's still way short of lifting it onto the wagon timbers. They'd be higher than the bed would have been."

Lyss, "Didn't need to. What I did was back the wagon over the slab. Again, loggers know to do this. With wedges I drove the stone up tight against the bottom and strapped it under my frame. The real trick was wending my way up out of the ravine without bottoming out. Getting it stuck one time would have put me in a real fix. By the time I pulled up in front of Doc Buckner's a crowd had formed behind the wagon. You'd have thought I'd bottled lightning."

Henry shook his head, "They can salute your genius; I'll salute your grit, or perhaps stubbornness, whichever the case may be. Now, let's have at it! Ledgers await!"

Ripley

"Cantankerous!" That would be the word Ulysses would favor to describe Reverend John Rankin. Some of the younger students at the Ripley Academy may prefer "spooky." The elderly man's lean frame and deep set eyes tended to lend credence to their judgment. Thin straight white hair and a booming voice were the things they noticed. The topics of his semi-monthly addresses were filled with convoluted theology that was more than they could take in.

Stories of escapades at his home high above on the brink of the hill abounded. They were filled with intrigue. These stories were always whispered, never told aloud. Shadowy figures had been seen slipping in and out during the night. People seem to have disappeared, never to be seen again. A legendary gunfight, others say "battle," once pierced a serene summer's night. Yet here he stands before them again expounding on the first chapter of John.

After his conclusion Reverend Rankin actually broke

a smile and softened his voice to the astonishment of all, "Seeing as the school term is nearing its close, and with the unusually mild climate we are experiencing, I have arranged with the trustees that classes shall be suspended tomorrow. There shall be chapel in the morning followed by a picnic."

And where was this picnic to be? At the academy? At the Presbyterian church? On the river bank? No! The picnic would be held at the Rankin home! It would be at a place that all students had wondered about, but nary a student ever dared to set foot. Students were filled with a curious mixture of excitement and dread. Anticipation would make it difficult to sleep that night.

John Rankin originally haled from Tennessee. There he had endeavored to obtain the best education available. Being from the most meager of means, he eventually worked his way up to and through seminary. Upon completion he promptly married the daughter of the esteemed head of the institution. He accepted the charge of a Presbyterian church and occasionally filled other pulpits of the region. However, due to his recurring theme that owning slaves was an abomination not only to the slaveholder, but also to the state and to the country as a whole, he was "invited to leave" the state of Tennessee.

He and wife Jean packed up their few possessions and headed for Ohio. Halfway along their route he sought temporary employment to secure enough funds to complete their journey. Consequently he was waylaid four years near Cane Ridge where the effects of a grand revival still lingered. He enjoyed strong support within his congregation, but fell out of grace with the surrounding community when he started a school for their slaves' children. Finally in 1822 he left his Carlisle, Kentucky congregation and again headed north. The exiled preacher completed his journey at Ripley, Ohio.

He found the little town to be like many others that were tucked in a narrow strip of bottomland between the river and lofty hills. The rough-and-tumble community was devoid of culture, devoid of acknowledgement of a higher calling. He gathered together a small congregation and nursed them along in the faith. They built a Presbyterian church of sound people and sound brick. He cajoled the citizens to put aside their waywardness. He fended off hecklers and even mobs to initiate churches in surrounding communities. He instilled cooperation with Methodists and Quakers to attain common goals. Eventually Ripley's saloons began to close. The distillery shut down. Industry grew. A large woolen mill and later a foundry provided employment for the townsfolk.

While he was finding success on the north side of the Ohio River, Rankin found disappointment on the south side. His brother Thomas bought a farm and its accompanying slaves only ten miles downstream at Augusta, Kentucky. He wrote Thomas a series of letters outlining his stance against slavery based on biblical, moral, and humanitarian principals. He then had his letters published in the Ripley *Castigator*. One by one other newspapers reprinted the series. Soon John Rankin was known far and wide as a leading philosopher of the anti-slavery movement. At a Zionsville convention he became one of the founders of the Ohio Anti-Slavery Society. He was frequently invited to address large audiences on the lecture circuit.

There were other trustees of the Ripley Academy that Ulysses attended that term, but everyone understood that it was Rankin's school. It was housed in a building intended as the new county court house. Ironically, the county seat was relocated to Lyss' hometown of Georgetown before the building was completed. After a short stint at an attempt as a college, the location became an academy for boys and girls. Winter terms began early in November and ran through most of March.

So it was Rankin's town. He appeared larger than life to the young students. They had all looked at the steps leading up, up, up from town. Up more than three hundred feet went the climb. Each hoped to one day make the grade and take in the view from high atop the hill. How wondrous it would be to stand above and look down upon the town, to take in the sweeping panorama of the magnificent river valley.

But accomplishing the summit would be to stand directly in front of Reverend John Rankin's house. It was no secret. Indeed it was a boast of the town. The Rankin house was a beacon to runaway slaves peering across from the Kentucky shore. Neither Rankin nor his sons would go into Kentucky to liberate a slave. However, any runaway who made it to his door was assured of swift passage north all the way to Canada. Any slave chaser discovered in Ripley was rudely escorted back whence he came. Any slave chaser who went prowling through the ravines or up on the hill did so at the risk of life and limb. Meeting up with a member of the Squirrel Hunters Club would not be a prosperous occasion. It was widely assumed that Rankin's older sons were "Squirrel Hunters."

The special picnic day started damp and cold down in the valley town. Chapel service commenced the day. Afterwards, half the girls and one boy elected to take the wagon on its circuitous route up. The remainder walked through morning fog to the end of Fourth Street. There they nervously huddled, wondering which of them would be brave enough to lead the way. Older boys had been assigned to lead groups of six. Ulysses, now in his sixteenth year, was among the leaders.

After a brief period of milling around, Ulysses took charge, "Alright! Everybody line up behind your leader." He stepped off long paces, "George, your group here! Paul, line yours over here!"

Soon the platoons were arranged. He looked towards the steps – nothing but fog.

"Stay close to your leaders, now! Follow me!"

A man suddenly appeared on the first step. Ulysses froze upon seeing the apparition. Normally he would have immediately recognized the Reverend. But the man was not in a pulpit, not on a speaker's platform. He was not in a clutch of dignified gentlemen. He was not in his dark suit. He wore the simple clothes of one doing farm chores.

Reverend Rankin welcomed the group, not in his lecture voice, but in a milder tone, "Good morning girls and boys." The students timidly mumbled replies. Rankin continued, "How are all of you on this sunshiny day? Oh, yes, it is sunny at the top. Just you wait and see. Take your time going up. It's a long way to go and not all of the steps are even. Do as Master Grant tells you and stay close to your leader. Here we go. Ulysses right after me, then each in turn."

With each step upwards the mist began to slip away. With each step upwards the students' fear and apprehension began to slip way. Sunbeams began to flutter round about. Chatter began to chase away quiet sullenness. Exhilaration gradually overtook somberness. Upon reaching the top each instinctively turned to see where the river should be. Up and down the entire length of the valley sunshine seemingly doubled its brightness from bouncing off a white pillow of fog. The Kentucky hilltops across the way were poking budding trees above the shimmering cloud. Dewdrops were twinkling at their feet.

Students gathered on the narrow strip of sod in front of the Rankin home. They were soon lined up behind their leaders. Ulysses checked his surroundings. His expectation of finding a fort of some fashion turned out to be quite an exaggeration. A modest house, a basic barn, and a few outbuildings surrounded by farm implements indicated a simple farmstead. An orchard, a chicken coop, a feedlot, and a garden currently covered in ragged stubble provided staples for the family. The story and a half brick house was not as large as it had appeared to be from below.

Then he saw it. It was about thirty feet east of the house. It was attached by rope and pulley to a twenty foot tall mast: the legendary lantern. It was brass with thick beveled glass and a reflector. Obviously it had been made for a steamboat, made to fend off wind and water. It was much larger and more luxurious than the simple tin lantern that Ulysses had supposed it to be. At times he had even doubted that it really existed. But there it was in all its glory basking in the sun. Now there was no doubt about it. The story had been told for years. The lantern would be lit and hoisted any night when Reverend John Rankin deemed that it was safe for runaway slaves to come to his farm. It could easily be seen from the Kentucky hills. Runaways are said to have shown up in spring, summer, fall, and winter – on dark nights, starry nights, moonlit nights – in fair weather and foul. By singles and droves they came. Some of Lyss' friends in Georgetown would always debunk the story. But here it was, the genuine item which confirmed the story. And its validation lent testimony to all the other tales told about the place. Ulysses was now a believer.

Pastor Rankin stepped in front of the group and pushed back his hat, "Is everybody accounted for? Yes, yes, good! Now you won't need to stay in these groups all day. We will all assemble here for lunch when the dinner bell rings and I would like to have you to eat with your group. Then late this afternoon the same again.

After which you will descend the steps with your group. Other than that, you can have your run of the place, outside that is. We have activities and games laid out for different ages."

He motioned to his children who stepped forward and lined up to the left of the group.

Pastor Rankin continued, "Now, for those of you who don't know, these are my children. They can help you get started. This is my youngest Lucy. She's five and she likes jumping rope. Next we have Billy and Andy. They will start off with the goat cart. MaryLiz will show off the baby animals. You can thank her for originating the idea for this school picnic. Johnny T. is going to head up a tug-o-war, followed by crack-the-whip, and then a horseshoe pitch. Julie will take some of you on a nature walk and then those who want to help set out lunch can give her a hand. How's that? Well, off you go!"

The small-fry scattered like geese being chased by a herd of puppies. Brief pandemonium quickly yielded to clutches of activity as enthusiastic schoolchildren adapted to the merry activities. Ulysses shook his head and gave a chuckle. He laughed at his own preconceived perception of the pastor and the house on the hill. Here he saw a tender father identifying with the interests of his children. The parent was encouraging the interests of each of his brood whether aged five or fifteen. The entire family had worked together to plan the day. Each had accepted responsibility for a portion of their program. The father set all in motion and allowed the children to share their interests with their guests. Julie he knew from school only as a polite, somewhat timid girl who was always reading. He knew that she was a "Rankin," but somehow his mind had never made a true connection of father-daughter.

What he had considered as only a place of refuge for forlorn sojourners was in actuality the home of a loving family. Ulysses wondered how such a large family could fit in the little house. But others thought the same about the Grant home when his aunt and cousins moved in. Jean Rankin, the mother, was undoubtedly busy inside preparing a feast. He knew that there were four older sons yet undetected. He was aware that the oldest son had completed his studies at Lane Seminary in Cincinnati and the second was currently enrolled at the same school. The next two boys, twins Samuel and Richard, were recent graduates of Ripley Academy in the class preceding Ulysses.

Laughter and shrieks told Ulysses that the students were all happily occupied. He headed for the horse stable. Rounding a long line of makeshift tables he heard someone calling him by name.

"Ulysses, over here! Lend a hand."

Looking to his left he saw the two strapping twins. He had seen them about town, but had never conversed with them. He wondered how they knew his name?

Samuel queried, "How about you taking over the crank? We've been turning this spit forever and there's still an hour to go!"

Ulysses was reluctant to get involved with the roasting pig that still looked like a pig. He felt trapped.

He had always managed to avoid the tannery and he constantly dodged his friends' hunting trips. This definitely seemed like another thing to be avoided. However, he could not turn down a direct plea from his host family.

"Sure," Lyss replied "show me what to do."

The boys gave him some tips on the process. Lyss found them to be quite congenial. This was a marked contrast to their quietly subdued character displayed around town. They freely conversed for a while before the two brothers headed for the barn. They pitched some hay down from the haymow then promptly disappeared for a half hour. Upon returning they discussed horses with Lyss for a spell. Finally Rich took the crank and Samuel raked the coals.

Rich commented, "I understand that you are a friend of Dan Ammen."

Lyss was surprised, "You know Dan?"

Rich explained, "Sure! Dan lived in Ripley before his family moved to Georgetown. They lived next door. His father David ran the newspaper."

Samuel interjected, "Don't you know? It was David Ammen that published our father's letters against slavery in the *Castigator*. Our father and Dan's father are two peas in a pod!"

Ulysses' mind jumped back to the night that Dan pulled him from White Oak Creek. Dan had suggested that their fathers were not only outspoken abolitionists but were also ushering runaways on their freedom quest. Now he had knowledge that directly linked them to

Reverend John Rankin. What else had Dan known, but not said?

Samuel Rankin set forth, "I noticed you eyeing the beacon pole earlier."

Lyss nodded nonchalantly.

Samuel, "We call it a 'Beacon of Hope.' We hold a dedication service for the lantern the first evening of each month, even if it is not to be lit that evening. We pray to the Lord that anyone who sees it and is in want of assistance will find hope and a sense of peace. We pray that the Lord will protect them and bring them to the light. The Lord has done mighty works with this little light."

Samuel spoke matter-of-factly. His tone was direct. Lyss heard phrases that he usually heard only while in church. However, he did not have the feeling that he was being preached at. Samuel was only relating his experiences.

Lyss admitted, "That brass lantern is more substantial than I had suspected. I mean, there are stories, second and third hand, practically legends, passed back and forth. No one can tell for sure which are fact and which are not." Ulysses knew that not all the stories ended in triumph. Some slaves were caught before reaching the northern shore of the Ohio River. Some drowned from mishaps, rickety boats, or breaking through the ice. Gunfire was not uncommon. Yet, if it is to be believed, hundreds upon hundreds overcame all obstacles to reach "Freedomland."

Samuel, "Certainly there are stories spread around.

In reality, there are more stories than can possibly be told. Powerful stories that will shake a man to his roots. Wondrous works that transform lives. The two of us have even seen slave chasers, the vilest of men, kneel with tears of repentance."

Rich slowly nodded in agreement as he attended the spit. He added, "It's been nearly six years since the British passed their anti-slavery law and Canada became a safe haven."

Samuel stoked the coals once again.

Samuel inquired, "What do you know about the Jordan River?"

Lyss did his best to show that Methodists knew the bible as well as any denomination. "The Jordan is over in the Promised Land. It flows from the Sea of Galilee down south to the Dead Sea. Moses was forbidden to cross the Jordan into the Promised Land because of a shortcoming. Joshua took the Israelites across on dry land and took the Battle of Jericho." He paused for a minute then added, "Jesus was baptized in the Jordan by John the Baptist."

Samuel nodded, turned slowly, then pointed south, "Isn't that a beautiful sight!"

Lyss turned to see. By now, the fog was completely gone. Sunshine was drenching all creation. His view of the silvery ribbon that was the Ohio River stretched for miles off to the west.

Lyss replied, "Yes! The French called it La Belle Riviere. I plan to do a sketch of it after lunch. I have several sketches of the river from a number of viewpoints. This certainly is a magnificent spot!" And it was. The view was even more superb than the one from the hill above Maysville.

Samuel continued, "Many of those who are drawn here by our beacon no longer call it the 'Ohio River.' They call the river that you are admiring the 'Jordan River.'" He paused for a slow deep breath, "According to them, you are standing in the 'Promised Land'!"

To The East

"You shall do no such thing!"

That was Mrs. Bailey's immediate response when Ulysses told her how he would be traveling from Georgetown to Ripley to begin his trip east. So now here he was in the back seat of the Bailey buggy with his travel bag at his side and his trunk strapped on behind. Dr. George Bailey kept mum while tending to the driving. He had been drafted for this outing. He would make the best of it by "consulting" with Dr. Wylie upon arrival at Ripley.

Mrs. Bailey turned in her seat to instruct Ulysses from her agenda. She had a number of things that she thought he ought to know about what lay ahead. She had been horrified when she had learned from Ulysses that neither of his parents intended to suitably "send him off." Lyss' plan had been to drive an old wagon down to the dock and leave it with an acquaintance. The rig could be picked up when the Grant Tannery made a delivery. The thought of Lyss "sneaking out of town like a criminal" irritated her – more so the more she thought on it. Yes, Hannah Grant seldom ventured out. Yes, she was expecting a child within months. Even so, she should have the courtesy of making the short trip to Ripley. Jesse Grant frequently traveled great distances on business. He had no excuse!

"I will not have you riding down there alone! The good doctor and I will drive you," she had told the neighbor lad. "We will have lunch at the hotel. If there is no boat heading upstream we will see to it that you have a room for however long is needed. I won't have it otherwise! So, there, it is settled!"

So it was settled. Not that Lyss minded. He always enjoyed Mrs. Bailey's company. As long as he could remember she had inquired about his endeavors. She appreciated his drawings. She was constantly well informed and had a creative bent of her own. She always had an extra muffin in the pie safe.

Table manners and hygiene were first on the list of instructions she had prepared for this trip. Etiquette was next: the protocol of formal introductions; conversation with elders; addressing ladies; the giving and accepting of mementos. This was followed by instruction on correspondence.

Ulysses accepted all of the advice. He was aware that Mrs. Bailey had traveled to Philadelphia on more than one occasion. She had selected her dinnerware and some of her household furnishings directly at the city's merchants. Of course, Philadelphia was the seat of culture for the entire continent.

"Now mind you," Mrs. Bailey continued, "just because you may not have been exposed to city life, don't you let anyone put you down. People there are no better than the people of Georgetown. Not as good in most cases; that's my opinion. They would be just as out of place here as you may feel to be there. Now, let me tell you about West Point."

Slowly the carriage descended the long slope towards the broad river. Mrs. Bailey ran out of things to say as the three approached the town on Second Street. Silently they passed the short blocks to Mulberry where they headed over to the Front Street landing district. Ulysses reflected on his time at the Ripley Academy. Now, only a few weeks after his seventeenth birthday, he realized that the year of 1839 was to be a demarcation for him – a year to separate "what was" from "what is to be."

Dr. Bailey turned the corner and pulled up to the handsome Bank Hotel. Ulysses caught a glimpse of the stacks of two steamers down the way. Stepping down from the carriage he caught a glimpse of a tear in Mrs. Bailey's eye.

Mrs. Bailey stood erect and announced, "Now then, we shall all have a fine luncheon at the Bank Cafe. Afterwards we shall see about your transport. Leave your bag until we know what's what." She looked young Ulysses over. His loose fitting newly homemade clothes were adequate, though plain. She had hoped that he could have had store clothes for his travels.

Lyss opened the door for his hosts. The two had just

passed when a firm boney hand came down on Lyss' shoulder. He jerked about.

"Well, I'll be jiggered! Look who I found!" Tevia shouted. "The little business man from Georgetown! Still a runt, are ya? Looks like yer keepin' pretty good company!"

Lyss, "Tevia! I knew something about that scrawny hand was familiar! You still with the *Clarion*? You going up or down? Is Patrick with you? Have you had lunch; can you join us? Tell me what you've been up to!"

The Baileys stepped back out onto the porch.

Lyss did the introductions, "Mrs. Bailey, Dr. Bailey, I would like you to meet Tevia, a friend of mine. Tevia runs things on the steamboat *Clarion*. Tevia, meet my neighbors from Georgetown, the esteemed Doctor Bailey and his charming wife."

The good doctor looked over the laborer outfitted in his work clothes. The boatman would be out of place at the best restaurant in town, but he invited, "Always glad to meet a friend of Ulysses. Won't you join us?"

Tevia, "Why, thank ya sir, but no time. Ya see, I was keepin' an eye out for Lyss, here. Our buddy Patrick met up with him here a month past when we were waylaid by low water and learned 'bout his goin' up the Hudson for military school and so the two of us were watchin' for him all over town hopin' he'd show up in time to catch passage with us. Well, how about it?"

The Baileys gave each other curious glances.

Lyss asked hopefully, "You're headed upstream? How far? When?"

Tevia, "Through to Pittsburgh! We've a full load of cotton on a tight schedule. There'll be short drop-offs at Marietta and Wheeling, but no dallying about! No taking on freight. But we gotta' move! We shove off at one o'clock! You know the Cap'n – one o'clock is one o'clock."

Mrs. Bailey exclaimed, "Oh, dear me! I had hoped for a leisurely day." She mustered cheerfulness, "My, it is certainly good fortune that we should happen to arrive just in time to catch your friends! Is it the first or second boat in line? No matter, the Doctor will take you all over to the wharf. I will have lunch for three sent if they can get it there in time. What is the name of the boat again?"

Tevia bowed, "Thank you ma'am! How kind of you. We will enjoy it. It's the *Clarion*, a fine ship and proud!"

Lyss turned to Mrs. Bailey, "Thank you for your kindnesses, today and over the years."

Mrs. Bailey began to sob. She nudged her husband. He gave her a quizzical look.

She tapped his vest pocket. "George, give it to him," she managed to say.

Dr. Bailey pulled a waxed paper from his pocket and unrolled it. "Here, for you, my boy. It's a fountain pen. It's from Birmingham, England, made of steel it is. I've used one like it for two years. This one's for you."

Lyss, "Thank you. It is quite handsome. That is very kind of you. I will make good use of it."

Mrs. Bailey, "I know that you will make all of Georgetown proud. Now off with you. God be with you." She kissed his cheek then turned quickly to the hotel door.

It was not long until the bell of the *Clarion* rang and the whistle sounded. The boat went into motion with Ulysses and his luggage safely on board. Patrick and Tevia leisurely went about their essential tasks. Ulysses stowed his belongings and began to adopt the unhurried rhythm of river life. He had paid the normal fare but had arranged with the captain to share in the crew's mess in exchange for light chores.

Patrick, Tevia, and Lyss carried their meal boxes out near the forecastle.

Patrick inquired, "Alright, Lyss, I rightly recall that you said that Ulysses was not your first name."

Lyss, "That's right. I am properly Hiram Ulysses Grant. I've always gone by Ulysses."

Patrick, "Your trunk clearly says 'UHG.' That doesn't jive."

Lyss, "Well, you've got me there. You see, Uncle Samuel Simpson over in Bethel put those brass tacks on for me as sort of a going away gift. He'd put on 'HUG' and asked if I was sure that that was what I wanted. Well, after seeing it I had to agree that 'HUG' might lead to some ribbing. So I let him change it. He promised not to tell Pa. Besides, no one knows me by Hiram."

Tevia, "Hug, ha! I see where you're comin' from on that. Hug, ha!"

Patrick inquired, "You told me about this military college thing when I saw you earlier, but I didn't follow it all. How does that work?"

Lyss, "Everyone calls it West Point, but that's its

location. Its title is the United States Military Academy. They train officers for the army."

Patrick, "Everyone has heard of West Point."

Tevia pondered, "Yeh, yeh, West Point, yeh, sure."

Patrick, "I never figured you for an army officer."

Lyss, "Well, Pa pointed out that you get four years of free college with special courses in mathematics and engineering. Once through, you serve another four years with the army then you're free to stay or go. Pa says he knows of three graduates who now are professors of mathematics at other colleges. That's a plan that makes sense to me."

Tevia, "Never heard of free college."

Patrick, "And they just hand this out?"

Lyss, "Well, there's a process. Mine was somewhat convoluted, though. You need to be appointed, normally by a congressman. You apply, he checks up on you, and if you pass muster he nominates you. When I get there I have to pass an examination. I'd rather eat nettles."

Patrick, "You'll do fine. If others can pass it, you can. So, how was your process convoluted, as you say?"

Lyss, "You saw that gentleman who delivered me to the wharf, didn't you? Well, Pa learned last Christmas that his son, a boy I grew up with, camped and fished and did everything with, was being expelled. Pa wrote to his friend Senator Tom Morris to suggest me as a replacement. Well, the senator did not have an appointment to give and sent the request to Representative Tom Hamer. Now both Morris and Hamer know Pa well from business, the lodge, and church and such. They both know me generally from around town. Pa and Hamer were close at one point, but they had a falling-out over Jackson politics and aren't on speaking terms. Anyway, Tom Hamer checked with the Georgetown school and the academies at Maysville and Ripley. He didn't run for reelection, so the story is the last thing he did in office before coming home was to give me the go-ahead. So off I go. Believe me, I'm in no hurry to get there."

Tevia, "Ah! It's in the stars that you go!"

Ulysses did not believe in stars. However, he did have an underlying sense of divine providence. Some things just had to be. There is no fighting destiny. Just like Hannibal, the woodchopper foreman who had a dream of his own plot of land, he would make the best of whatever situation he landed in. Hannibal now has a cozy home with a little farm and is a carpenter in demand.

Patrick, "Let me get this straight. Your friend gets the boot and you get dropped into his place by a man who is mad at your Pa and may not have gotten it done if he had not gone in on his last day of work and then the friend's father drives you to our boat and buys a fine lunch for us all. That about it?"

Lyss, "If any good comes of this, Pa and Mr. Hamer will reconcile and Bart Bailey will get back on the straight and narrow."

Tevia, "Things will work out for you. You have sense enough – and gumption. Just like when you got the goods on that conniving rapscallion that we had walk the plank."

They all had a good laugh at the thought of LeMunyon sloshing through mud up to his knees.

By the second day Ulysses adapted to the ship's routine. He pulled out two books he had brought: *Algebra Fundamentals* and *The Last of The Mohicans*. The latter was a gift from Grandma Simpson. The former was recommended by Reverend Rankin. Apparently the Reverend knew something about the West Point appointment before he did. Perhaps the good reverend had been contacted directly by the Honorable Thomas Hamer.

Reverend Rankin had told Ulysses, "We have no one here to teach algebra. You will need to know it one day." He had told Ulysses where he could purchase it in Cincinnati. "You have an uncanny capacity for mathematics; you can handle it."

Try as he might, algebra was a chore. He could come up with answers to the problems in his head, but the explanations in the text were gibberish. He found that Cooper's novel fit the mood of his trip much better. It fed his adventurous spirit. Adventure would be his theme.

Upon arrival at Marietta, Patrick gave Ulysses a brisk tour of the town: the waterfront; the business district; and the shipyards on the Muskingum River. Ulysses inquired about the historic sites. They went to the Indian mound. They poked around the old Campus Martius district where Arthur St. Clair had governed the original Northwest Territory. They peeked into the window of Rufus Putnam's former home. There was no time to cross the Muskingum to Harmartown to investigate the point that once held the long-gone historic Fort Harmar. They had to forgo Marietta College.

Captain Hendricks seemed bent on record time making it up to Pittsburgh. No explanation was asked and none was given. The Ohio River continued its enchantment with even higher hills to the left and to the right. Ulysses took in the amazing sight of the approach to Pittsburgh where the river grew wider and wider. The Allegheny River approached from ahead on the left while the Monongahela approached from ahead on the right. At a point at the bottom of the city, the two met at a point which Captain Hendricks referred to as Mile Zero. From this point all navigation charts for the Ohio River were numbered.

As soon as the *Clarion* landed at a pier on the Allegheny side, Ulysses headed for the location of Fort Pitt which once overlooked the point. On this spot the British had set up a small outpost which was superseded by the French Fort Duquesne. The point went back to the British and then to the Americans. Ulysses found earthworks defining a good portion of the former stronghold. The remains of one old stone blockhouse had been remade into a residence.

An easy walk to the east led into the city. He located Western University on Third Street. He entered the stout three-story stone building and hung around a while to see what he could absorb. Following Smithfield Street up to Liberty he viewed tightly packed shops of every sort. Taking a right on Liberty he soon came to the Canal

Basin, the western terminus of the Pennsylvania Canal Works. The system was an engineering marvel transporting passengers and goods all the way to Philadelphia by way of two canals and two railroads.

Ulysses arranged his passage and hired an Irish boy with a dolly cart. Together they walked back to the *Clarion* to claim his baggage. The way led along the Allegheny through a row of foundries and other heavy industry. "Hard working people in a no-frills town," he summed it up. He was disappointed to find Patrick and Tevia had disappeared into the city. He found the Captain at the fore of the top deck leaning on the rail while peering down upon the unloading. The man was slowly puffing on his pipe with a very satisfied look on his face. Ulysses congratulated him on the successful voyage and gave his farewell.

Ulysses embarked on the second leg of his many faceted journey. He found the canal boat to be surprisingly strong and comfortable. It operated something like a miniature riverboat carrying a variety of goods along with a variety of passengers. But it was a riverboat that had lost its paddle with its pounding and steam engine with its accompanying heat, smoke, and constant demand for tending. He found the canal boat to be eerily quiet – skimming along without apparent effort. He calculated that if he cleared it out he could load fifteen wagonloads of wheat into the boat.

Nothing had prepared him for crossing the Allegheny River on a long aqueduct. Only three blocks from the Canal Basin where he had boarded, before he had a chance to settle in, he found himself gliding high above the river on a man-made creek in the sky. "Weird," he thought. He found the leisurely pace, the smooth ride, the comradery of fellow passengers, the view of the farm fields and running brooks all to his liking. He could have traveled faster on the stage line, but no, this was the way to go. He studied each lock, each dam, and each and every aqueduct over every nameless creek coming from whatsoever direction. At spells he would walk the towpath in shine and shade keeping pace with the boat, at times conversing with the mule driver.

The next leg of the journey was by railroad, another mode that he had never experienced. The railcar had a sway that was a bit unsettling at first. Not the jostling of a wagon, but a peculiar twitch and bump. He sat near the front to admire the steam engine on wheels. After an hour or so on the rail line a station was reached. Everyone got out and all were transferred to incline cars. Yeomen unloaded and reloaded the goods and baggage. The incline cars on incline tracks were pulled uphill an elevation of two hundred feet or more by a cable powered by a stationary steam engine at the top. As they went up, another group of cars passed them going down. At the top there was a transfer to another railroad section. On it went – five railroads, five inclines, and yes, one tunnel.

Ulysses acknowledged that he was getting the full measure of adventure he sought. The engineering was fabulous. The accommodations were remarkable. The view was marvelous. The station at the summit of the mountain ridge included a grand tavern and hotel. Here passengers could take a respite. Ahead lay five inclines down with accompanying railroad sections between. Then would come another canal, this one much longer than the first. Finally at Columbia they would board the final leg, the Philadelphia and Columbia Railroad zipping along at better than fifteen miles every hour.

The entire trip was exhilarating for young Ulysses. It was like he had entered a new world. It was almost enough to make him forget about entrance examinations.

Bethel Summer

Sarah Simpson strode quickly to a bench at Harrisburg's canal depot. She bent slightly and addressed her companion, "The captain is determined to leave the dock promptly at one o'clock as posted. Every other boat I have ever dealt with is always delayed and delayed again. But, no, our boat must be prompt this time! We will never make connections with Ulysses. There are no other trains arriving from Philadelphia until late in the day. I don't see any way for him to make it here on time. I simply cannot stay over one more day. We will proceed without him!"

Kate Lowe replied, "Let's walk up to the Capitol Building again. Maybe your grandson is somewhere in the crowd along State Street. Maybe he is waiting on the front steps of the capitol instead of this side. We can find a vendor and eat a clerk's lunch on the capitol grounds and keep an eye out." She added cheerily, "We'll still have plenty of time to return here; maybe he'll be on this very spot when we get back."

Sarah agreed, "Yes, one more time. It's too boisterous here anyway. It is a pleasant day for a stroll. Come along."

Kate observed that the sixty-eight year old lady never "strolled." Sarah's steps were always quick and sharp as if urgent business needed attending. The woman had led a rural life, but when she was in the city it was the city that was intimidated, not her. Kate followed along through heavy street traffic, pockets of construction, residences intermingled with shops, and three cross-streets. The bustling avenue gave way to a park-like government center for the state of Pennsylvania. Up the hill towards the tall red brick building they went for the third time this morning. Actually, the stately government house stood only two stories. It looked much taller due to it sitting on a hill. Columns on a curved portico and additional columns on a domed tower added to the illusion. Sarah kept glancing at the tower clock. On the top step she stopped and turned. She studied the pedestrians, looking to find anyone familiar. The two of them sat together on a pedestal on the portico. A mild breeze drifted across the early June air.

Sarah Simpson confided in her newfound friend, "Thank you for your patience while I completed my transaction. I just could not leave Pennsylvania without having the final 'i' dotted and the final 't' crossed. The nature of my journey was to dispose of a plot of ground that my John had inherited years back up in Horsham Township. That's a little over fifteen miles north of your home in Philadelphia. The judge in Norristown suggested that I bring my papers here to the state capital to get untangled. While back in Philadelphia and surroundings, I made some social calls. I visited relatives whom I had corresponded with over the years since I married and moved west. I have visited back East twice and my sister visited Ohio once.

"As you know, your lawyer uncle in Bethel placed me in contact with your father's Philadelphia law office. Without their services my trip would have been all for naught. As it now stands, all is a success, the bonus being meeting such a sweet young lady as yourself. And now we are fast friends off to the western country of Ohio." She gave a chuckle, "You're told that you are to look after me and I'm told to watch over you.

"My first journey to Bethel was much different. It was thirty-three years ago – no canal, no railroad then. We packed our wagon, children and all, at Horsham, bade farewell and pointed west. Wending our way through those mountains we came out at Wheeling. There we sold the wagon and bought a half-share in a flatboat. Tumbling down the Ohio River we went." She raised a pointed finger, "More than once we were saved by the sheer strength of my husband! We glided into Point Pleasant, Ohio and, after a short trek north, there we were. John had an enchanting home and farm waiting for us.

"Of course I was much older than you are now. But never mind, I am sure you will find adventure enough during your summer visit. I only wish Ulysses could have joined us."

After a deep breath and a brief spell she continued, "I miss my John. He was a good provider, respected around Bantam and Bethel. He took pride in his farm and was a good steward of the ground. He always looked out for those who needed a helping hand. A good Christian man, he was. Now he lies in the lovely Methodist cemetery north of Bantam not far from the ground he worked. Don't get me wrong. We are Presbyterian!" She added with a sly grin, "But whatever the denomination, we all get along once we are in the ground.

"I moped and pitied myself for two full years. Ulysses' departure for the Military Academy shook me again. I wasn't prepared for it. He has always been such an inspiration. One Sunday after church services I said to myself, 'Self, you've had a good life and it is far from over. The Good Lord has things he still wants you to do. Stand up straight and get about living.' This I did. This trip is one result.

"Don't tell anyone this, Kate, but when I reached Philadelphia it was all I could do to keep from continuing on to West Point. Now wouldn't that have been embarrassing to a young man to have his grandmother come to college and tuck him into bed at night? Anyway, it's been two years and a month since I laid eyes on that boy and every hour of delay hurts."

Kate nodded sympathetically. The Sarah Simpson that she was becoming acquainted with was full of energy and vigor. She was interesting and knowledgeable, fun to be with.

Sarah suggested, "Kate, would you go around to the front portico and look from there while I watch for Ulysses from here?"

Kate was somewhat astonished, "How would I know what to look for? I don't know him and he doesn't know me. I'm not sure that I would be of any good service."

Sarah instructed, "He is to be in uniform. He isn't very tall. His walk is more of a saunter with a slouch, like a farmer walking across plowed ground."

Kate, "And what does a West Point uniform look like?"

Sarah, "Well, I don't rightly know. Like a regular Army officer's uniform, I suppose: blue jacket, white pants, cap of some sort."

Kate, "Like that one down there by the lamp post?"

Sarah, "Likely so. But that can't be Ulysses, too erect, too tall."

Kate, "Perhaps, but the Army hangs together. He may know your grandson and his whereabouts. Let's ask."

Sarah, "No, no, I couldn't."

Kate stated, "I can!"

Kate Lowe ran off to meet the fine looking young military officer.

"How audacious young ladies are nowadays," Sarah thought to herself, "unabashedly approaching a young man!" She peeked at the conversation below while still searching the crowd. She had hoped that Ulysses could meet this girl who was on summer leave from her finishing school. Sarah was keenly aware of Lyss' shyness around pretty girls. With both of the young students having several weeks in Bethel without responsibilities, perhaps romance could flourish. But Ulysses was not to be found and Kate was meeting a handsome young officer.

Kate began waving excitedly, motioning for Sarah to join them. Sarah approached cautiously. The officer turned to greet her. Could it be? It was!

"Grandma Simpson!" Cadet Ulysses S. Grant called out with outspread arms.

After hurried greetings, introductions, a bite to eat, and packing Ulysses on board, the three settled in for the journey west. The *Iroquois* shoved off two hours late. But what was two hours to a spring day on a canal. Kate and Ulysses were soon in deep conversation, oblivious to their surroundings, unaware of Grandma Simpson and the other passengers. They talked about their respective schools, instructors, facilities, schedules. They chatted about novels and art. Sarah pulled out yarn that she had purchased in Philadelphia. She arranged it on her lap and began knitting a mitten for her Christmas stash. She kept one ear bent.

Ulysses was obviously taken in by Kate's natural beauty and soft smile; she by his blue-grey eyes and easy manner, and yes, by his uniform. Lyss knew that he was backward by nature. He was a wallflower at Academy dances and banquets. But he had learned by observation, especially from his friends from the South. James Longstreet, from the class ahead and known to all cadets as "Pete", was especially adept socially. Lyss mentored Pete in math and Pete included Lyss in his social circles. Lyss was determined that this summer he would not retreat. He could do this thing.

Upon finishing her second mitten Sarah interjected, "Now Lyss, you sit here by your grandmother and tell her all about your progress. I appreciate your letters, good letters at that, but I want to know all about what you have gone through."

Lyss shifted to his left and addressed her directly, "Of course, Grandma. I stayed the extra day until standings were posted. I stand twenty-fourth in my class of fifty-three. So I am in the top half. I'm sorry if my delay caused any distress. I just had to know the postings."

Sarah agreed, "I'm certain that I would have done the same given the circumstances."

Lyss added, "Circumstances also allowed for me to meet up with Dan Ammen while passing through Philadelphia. That was a grand opportunity that I couldn't let pass. He is such a solid friend. We talked for several hours in the lobby of the Jones Hotel on Chestnut Street. We had a magnificent time. I'm afraid that I let it carry on a little too long – that's why I did not arrive here yesterday."

"All is forgiven. Your time couldn't have been better spent than seeing Dan," Sarah told her grandson. She then asked, "Tell me Lyss, how many were there when your classes began the first year?"

Lyss, "Sixty even."

Sarah, "So you are twenty-fourth out of sixty. Now, how many candidates were there in the preliminary camp before entrance?"

Lyss, "Ninety-seven candidates were nominated and showed."

Sarah, "So you are twenty-fourth out of ninety-seven. That's much better than half, wouldn't you say? Remember how terrified you were before the entrance examination and how surprised you were at its ease. Two years later it's a thing of the past and you have forgotten all about it. Now you are practically in the top quarter of the bunch."

"Yes, ma'am," Lyss agreed.

Sarah, "Your letters tell me that you fare better in mathematics than in language, is that correct?"

Lyss beamed, "This term I posted tenth in mathematics. My professor on occasion has me present my solution for the class." He allowed this one opportunity to put his modesty aside, mostly for his grandmother, partly for the girl beside him. Actually, the professor had often celebrated his mathematical ingenuity during class.

Scattered layers of fog surrounded the canal on the morning of the second day. Sarah sat beside her grandson at the fore of the canal boat and covered herself with a blanket. Bands of Jersey dairy cows grazed in pastures on both sides as the vessel silently glided past.

Sarah said to Lyss, "My cousin Elizabeth told me about your stay in Philadelphia on your trip east to the Military Academy. She said you were the perfect house guest. She told how you visited all the historic places that I had charted for you. Walk me the two years from there to where we are now. You told me about your academics. Tell me about what you experienced."

Lyss understood that here was the one person he could confide in wholeheartedly. Of this he had been deprived for a long time.

He delved in, "West Point is a trove of history. Its strategic location guarded the Hudson River during the Revolution. All the famous generals were there at one time or another. Unfortunately, Benedict Arnold is the name that everyone first connects with West Point. The Hudson is beautiful. Dare I say as beautiful as the Ohio? I can sit at the overlook across from the parade grounds and picture war ships under sail silently sweeping up from the right around the bend. On Sunday afternoons I climb the hill to the west where there are remnants of Fort Putnam, a Revolutionary War fortress that protected the landward approach to the main fort. Often I sit and read, sometimes I sketch the view. I have to admit that I read more Washington Irving and James Fenimore Cooper than I do my science and French assignments."

Sarah reinforced an earlier history lesson, "No doubt the fort on the hill was named after Rufus Putnam who founded Marietta, Ohio and was sent by President Washington to old Fort Washington in Cincinnati and on to Vincennes to hold councils with the Indians."

Lyss responded, "Yes, the same Putnam. He engineered a number of forts up and down the Hudson." He approached a touchy subject, "At the Academy I am known as 'Sam.' Nobody calls me Hiram nor Ulysses."

Grandmother Sarah gave him a quizzical look at this revelation.

Lyss continued, "At the initial call they called for Ulysses S. Grant – Ohio. I protested that that was not my name. The man replied that according to the United States Army it was. I tried during my first term to straighten things out. All attempts were useless. So I started as Hiram Ulysses Grant; I planned to become Ulysses H. Grant; but now I must be Ulysses S. Grant. Apparently Tom Hamer wrote it that way on my nomination."

Sarah chuckled, "The 'S' for Simpson, no doubt. It wouldn't surprise me if he had never heard you called Hiram. I don't understand about Sam."

Lyss, "All cadets are given nicknames by upperclassmen. U.S. Grant became Uncle Sam as a joke for them and now Sam I am. Most of the corps know me by that name and no other. I don't think that will be acceptable to father."

Sarah, "It was my John that came up with Hiram. I pushed for Ulysses and your father seconded it. I don't think Sam fits you at all. As you know, your brother Sim is actually Samuel Simpson Grant. No, no, one Sam in your family is enough for me."

Lyss confided, "The first year was very tough and not just because of the courses. If Dan Ammen's older brother Jake, the one who as a lieutenant was on the faculty at West Point and now teaches in Kentucky, hadn't given me insights on how they conspire to break

[155]

down plebes, well, I might just have packed up and headed for home like some others did. That and the idea that I was scared to death of coming home a failure made me stick. There was some talk in Congress about abolishing the Academy. I followed the debates thinking that that could be my out. The second year proved more accommodating and now I'm determined to do my best to see it through. Not that I intend to continue a military career after my obligation, but it's my best chance for a top education. I see now that Pa was right about that. I'm thinking I may want to become a mathematics professor some day like Jake. There are plenty of respectable men who have left the Army after the Academy, but who would be ready to serve in a time of crisis."

Sarah saw that the boy that left Georgetown was now an adolescent who was fast heading towards manhood. Could she let go of the boy?

Sarah commented, "I suppose the Army has reasons for the way they do things." They sat quietly for a moment. She asked, "What brings you joy?"

Lyss responded brightly, "I took to reading novels and poetry. My painting class was interesting. My painting techniques have improved, though not the best. I brought along some samples. I'll let you select one for yourself."

Sarah, "I would love that. We will need to wait for a dry day to get them out."

Lyss continued, "What really improve the Academy this year was that they introduced riding into the curriculum and into maneuvers. Somehow that had been neglected in the past. I began hanging around the stables and volunteering to help out here and there. The sergeant in charge of the animals, a practical sort of a fellow, let me work the horses and break the ones that were still rough. I guess that's the one area in which I've distinguished myself amongst my classmates."

Grandmother Sarah's eyes brightened. She exclaimed, "Thank you Lord! It's an answer to prayer! I've prayed and prayed for the Lord to send you some horses. You've never mentioned it in your letters!" She patted his knee.

The two sat quietly as the boat stopped at a mule changing station. The sun began to poke through a layer of dense clouds. An old man hawked some apple butter and small loaves of bread. The driver efficiently completed the exchange, took the slack out of the tow rope, and again set the pace.

Sarah inquired, "I can tell there's something else that you have not told me. Something is troubling you, Lyss."

Lyss hung his head, "I've, I've started having headaches that knock me flat. Nobody knows. I've hidden it. If they learn that I have a mental disease, I will be promptly discharged. There's no two ways about it. I have been getting demerits for being late to roll call. When pressed for a reason, I say that I had been drinking too much. This they tolerate to some degree."

Sarah sighed, "Oh, Ulysses, you just broke my heart!" She stifled a tear. "All these years I have never truly been able to help your mother overcome her maladies. No matter how we try, people never understand what she's going through. Now this! Oh, you poor boy! So full of promise!"

Lyss encouraged her, "It's alright. I have managed it. I am determined that no one will ever know! I will hide it through thick and thin! Now enough of this; let's get some lunch. And you have more knitting to do if you are to fill your secret bin for Christmas!"

Sarah laughed, "Well, I guess my secret bin isn't such a secret after all, is it?"

He tried to dismiss haunting thoughts from his mind. Still he remembered how once when he was alone with his mother she said, and only once, and he never forgot, "When the feeling creeps over my mind, like the Devil reaching out his hand, fear of losing control is worse than the happening. Surrendering, I trust the Lord that He will bring me back."

Upon arrival at New Richmond, young Ulysses found it odd that he would be one of the passengers to be shuttled to Bethel. In the past he had always been the one driving the wagon. In this case Grandma Simpson had sent word for her step-son Samuel to fetch them in a proper buggy. While waiting for their ride Lyss pointed out to Kate the few local landmarks. He presented her with a watercolor of a Moorish marketplace. Samuel first took his mother to the Bantam farm. From there he took the young pair into Bethel: Kate to her Uncle John Lowe's home and Lyss to the Grant's new home.

Jesse Grant had moved from Georgetown to gain a larger tannery in Bethel. He now had forty vats to work the hides. The location provided easier access to markets and shipping in Cincinnati by eliminating the obstacle of White Oak Creek Canyon. He moved his family into a two story brick home which he purchased from Senator Tom Morris. The roomy house faced the stage stop across Bethel Pike.

Jesse was proudly waiting for his son. He held the bridle of a prized horse, "He's an unbroken colt, just the way you like them. I selected him specifically for your summer use. I am told that his sire could outrun his shadow."

Inside, mother Hannah presented the newest Grant, baby Mary, soon to be two years old. "You look taller," summed up his mother's greeting. Brother Sim was gone on business, sisters Clara and Virginia presented him with his favorite muffins, and little brother Orvil hid behind the parlor door.

Daily rides were in order. First to Georgetown to visit Mrs. Bailey and Mrs. Betsy King he went. Then out to the King farm he rode. An air of apprehension crept over him as he approached. His hesitation was swept away when he saw Lucy snipping some hollyhocks beside the front porch. She turned and waved excitedly. He saw that she had her horse saddled ready to ride.

Lucy greeted, "I knew you would come! I just knew it! Come in and say 'hello' while I put together a picnic lunch. Let's see, you'll want a smidgen of honey for your cornbread, won't you? Where would you like to go? I know a meadow upstream from New Hope where buttercups are in bloom. You know, just below the pawpaw patch. How long will you be visiting? Do you need a fresh horse? I want you to tell me all about the East."

Indeed it was a good day for riding and a picnic. It was a good day for wildflowers and bees. It was a good day for young romance.

Ulysses spent most summer days riding to Georgetown, Bantam, Batavia, and smaller villages visiting relatives and friends. Many of those days were spent with either Kate or Lucy. Kate he found to be interested in reading and writing poetry. She enjoyed shopping in Cincinnati for Spanish silver jewelry. She preferred being driven in a carriage to riding. She dreamed of Paris and London. Lucy loved all things out of doors. She was eager to ride the countryside. She walked the woods, waded streams, rescued injured animals. She could harness a team and hitch it to a wagon. She talked about every baby in the neighborhood. She wanted eight children. She dreamed of a cottage by a stream with sheep and goats and dogs.

Independence Day 1841 in Georgetown was less than the usual rousing affair. William Henry Harrison, the regional hero whose election campaign dominated the scene only one year previous, had died precisely three months before this year's lackluster celebration. That was exactly one month after his inauguration as President. The savior of the west was gone. Last fall's campaign mementos brandishing depictions of log cabins and hard cider were displayed once again, this time draped with black mourning ribbons. President Tyler was currently making the local constituency nervous.

The lack of luster did not halt all celebrating. Ulysses was looked upon as the local hero for the day. He seemingly shook every hand in town. That night he retired his uniform for the remainder of his stay. He had grown tired of wearing it daily; it was stifling in the summer's heat; he wanted to distance himself from the Academy during the remainder of his vacationing; his mother thought it to be pretentious.

The only cool place to be found on the second Monday of August was deep within White Oak Creek Canyon. The canyon was a peaceful place where memories best lingered. Ulysses and Lucy met at what had been Lyss' favorite camping site beside the creek. Rays of the late summer sun filtered down through tall trees. The creek ran at a mere trickle. Squirrels scurried about with little bursts of commotion.

Lyss spoke softly, "Right over there is where Dan Ammen yanked me from the creek. It's hard to imagine that it was a raging torrent capable of destruction."

Lucy held his hand, "Yes, I know. Come, show me where you gathered up Dr. Buckner's famous rock stoop."

They clamored two hundred yards upstream. They removed their boots and waded through cool water to a shallow pool

Lucy examined the space with her toes, "Yes, I feel it. Here's one corner. Come here and hold my hands." He quickly obeyed. "Now hear what I have to say." She put on her best smile, "It has been a splendid summer. Why should it end? Why should you go out East? You can stay with me. Father says you can work for him. You can take a room with Aunt Betsy. Once settled you can start up a freight business again. Georgetown is where you belong."

Ulysses protested, "I must return to the West Point! I have no choice. I signed an oath. It's my duty; a thing of honor! You know that I will not be back here for two years. After that I will have four years obligation to the Army. I can be assigned anywhere, moved about at their whim. Only after that will I be my own man. I am not sure I can be the one in your cottage beside a stream."

Lucy lowered her chin, "I can wait for you."

Ulysses knew better. She was still an impetuous girl that could not set aside her notions. He was aware of several boys wishing he would leave town and quit turning the heads of the local girls. He squeezed her hands while he contemplated a response.

Lyss made a promise, "If I return two years hence and you are not married and forming your family of eight children, then I will meet you right here and we will take up where we are now."

"I will wait for you," she promised.

West Point

May of 1843 brought a fine show of tree blossoms to the Hudson Valley heralding a promise of new beginnings. June broke warm and inviting. On the twenty-first day of the month the river at West Point was filled with sailboats and steamers bringing guests to the Academy dock. With an air of excitement visitors ascended the long winding path up to the parade grounds.

Fife and drum filled the air as the Corps of Cadets presented Dress Parade to onlookers. The Corps stood at attention as distinguished alumni were introduced. Young Ulysses' mind wandered back to the first parade he had witnessed on these grounds. Back then he did not even have a uniform. General Winfield Scott, Commanding General of the Army, impressed Candidate Grant as the epitome of soldiering. The superbly uniformed old warrior on a large gray speckled steed burned an image of admiration into his mind. Today, many parades later, he allowed a feeling of satisfaction to creep over him.

Upon dismissal at completion of the ceremonies, Cadet First Class Frederick Dent searched out his roommate. He was well aware that Ulysses had a habit of disappearing during social events. He thought his classmate and friend should relish this day to its fullest. He was surprised to see him near a platform where a military band was playing martial music. Rufus Ingalls was introducing "Sam" Grant and "Sly Bob" Hazlitt to family members from Maine. Fred joined the party and together they strolled about the campus, stopping here and there to sip punch and munch on crumpets and jam. When shadows lengthened across the walkways the Ingalls family took their leave. Fred and Lyss hastened towards their room.

Fred took his friend by the arm, "Sam, I know that you won't be attending tonight's ball, but I would like you to stop in for a while. Just to meet and greet, then you can step out. Time is short and who knows where we go from here."

Lyss begged out, "Thanks for inviting, but I can't. I need to prepare for tomorrow."

Fred, "I know. Here I am fancy free, but you have one more duty to perform. I dare say, it is being whispered all about that something big is in store for tomorrow. I'm bringing everyone that I know."

The following afternoon Fred and friends were on the front row in the Equestrian Hall, known as "Horse Palace" to cadets. An equestrian demonstration had been added as an afterthought to the previous year's graduation displays. This year it was part of the regular second day program alongside artillery, rifle marksmanship, and fencing demonstrations. At the equestrian hall participating cadets forsook their dress uniforms in favor of loose fitting and somewhat drab riding suits. Makeshift bleachers overflowed with spectators; viewers jostled for standing room. The crowd, already in a party mood, cheered as riders masterfully maneuvered through their drills. Following a short intermission, half the platoon gave demonstrations of their skills with mounted swordsmanship. Hurdles were set up and the second half began a variety of jumps.

Fred stepped out to go looking for his roommate. Ulysses had been excused after the grand entrance. He was at the warm-up arena outside. He was stroking a huge muscular chestnut bay horse.

Lyss spoke in a soft monotone, "Well, York, it's just you and me. We've come a long way since we first met; you have and I have, both of us. One more duty and then graduation. We'll do this thing together. We're a team, you and I. We'll make our mark and be bound together forever by it."

He gave York a slice of apple. He worked his way back alongside the animal and ran his hand along the cinch. He inspected the saddle rigging, all the while chatting with a soothing voice. He took hold of the bridle and walked York in a figure eight path. He stopped abruptly and looked into the left eye of the steed, "It is our day! We will do it up right!"

Fred was standing quietly off to the side. He stepped

up. He came closer than he had ever been to the fiery horse. Even after nearly two years of Ulysses' training, York still had a fierce intimidating look. Early on, Sergeant Herschberger, Academy Horse Master, was prepared to ship the beast out. Everyone was afraid to go near him, let alone ride him. Only Lyss' continual interventions kept him on duty. One more duty and he would be the star of the day, and yes, of the three days' events.

Fred interjected, "Yes, Sam, it's your day! You've stayed in the shadows long enough. You don't know it, but you are already a legend among our classmates because of your horsemanship, way beyond the rest of us. This day will attest to it to everyone else. I'm proud of you – I just wanted to let you know. I've got to get to my seat; you'll be up soon."

Sergeant Herschberger yelled from across the way, "Mount up, Grant! At the ready!"

Lyss replied to his classmate, "Thanks, Fred. We're ready! See you afterwards."

The main hall emptied of riders. One hurdle was placed to the right of the center of the arena at the standard forty-two inch height. The program announcer held up his megaphone and called out, "Cadet Grant riding York!"

Ulysses leaned forward and whispered in York's left ear, "Now's the time, step lively."

He patted his mount on the shoulder and nudged his knees against the barrel of York's ribs. York darted into the stadium. The crowd sat in silent expectation. Three times horse and rider cantered around the arena, each time gathering speed. The fourth time the hurdle was approached and cleared in stride. Polite applause was granted.

Sergeant Herschberger signaled with a cane to have the bar raised. This was promptly attended to by two stablemen. Lyss waved to the sergeant. Herschberger in turn signaled with his cane and the bar was raised a second notch. Three times around the ring Lyss and York went, this time at a quicker pace. The approach, the leap, the clearance were accomplished in perfect order.

Once again the sergeant had the bar raised. Once again Lyss waved it off. The bar was raised another notch higher. Herschberger walked out and made a show of inspecting the equipment. He stood erect and deliberately walked under the bar to emphasize the height. He returned to his position and pointed to Ulysses. Three times around, with greater speed each lap, with greater anticipation by the spectators, with hubbub escalating, a quickened pace was obtained. York's eyes flared. Ulysses showed neither change of stance nor expression. York turned at the head of the hall. The jump was initiated without any adjustment to stride. The gallery went quiet one instant and broke into acclamation the next.

"Amazing!" "I wouldn't have thought it possible!" "I've never seen anything like it!" "A horse and a half, that is!"

Ulysses took one lap at pace and one at a walk. He gave a salute to the sergeant and left whence he came.

The stablemen ran to the hurdle and measured the center of the bar with a tape measure. The taller of the two raised a white flag. Herschberger strode to his assistants then to the announcer.

The announcer raised his megaphone, "A new record for the Academy! Five feet, six and one-half inches! The mark will be submitted to the New York state association for national recognition!"

Fred rushed to the outside arena where he found Ulysses walking York, "You did it! It looked so easy, powerful yet smooth! They'll put your name up on the Horse Palace wall for that. It'll be there for an easy twenty years, maybe fifty! Shoot, they may as well set it in stone!"

A throng headed their way from the Equestrian Hall. Lyss was still in his horse training mind frame. York still needed attention for his cool-down.

"Thanks, Fred," he replied mildly. "See if you can keep that crowd back. York won't stand for being mobbed. Somebody could get hurt."

Fred chuckled to himself. As typical, Lyss would see his business through before celebrating. Accolades would have to wait.

Fred turned to face the onrush, "Easy folks! Quiet down and hold back! Give Cadet Grant some time to settle his mount. I suggest that nobody wants to get too close while York is skittish." He edified those who did not know, "That is Cadet First Class Ulysses S. Grant!"

Flags fluttered in a warm southern breeze the next afternoon. All of the guests were in their finest regalia.

The Corps of Cadets were in rank and file for the culmination of the three-day festivities: Graduation Exercises. On the schedule was promotion of underclassmen, graduation of the class of 1843, recognition of graduates at the grade of Lieutenant Second Class (brevet), United States Army.

Ulysses glanced to his left and to his right at his classmates. The four years at West Point seemed like an eternity. In another sense, they had passed rather quickly. He had come principally to get the degree that would be handed to him today; a certificate that would serve him for life. During this time of reflection he realized that lessons he had learned at this hallowed institution were the greater prize. Yes, he could have studied harder; but then he would not have been true to himself. He had not altered his character to please others. He had neither lied, nor cheated, nor connived, nor put on airs, nor done anything to tarnish his honor.

He realized, too, that four years ago he had come to please his father, relatives, even the people of Georgetown. These obligations had diminished while the comradery of his classmates had grown. They had grown into a brotherhood. It was in this fraternity of fellow officers that he was proud to be counted as a member. He was pleased that he was in good standing with each and every one.

Ulysses, Fred Dent, Bob Hazlitt, and Rufus Ingalls wasted no time putting the celebration behind them. Together the comrades headed for New York City. The jaunt was partly business and partly pleasure. The first order of business was to forward their trunks to their homes. Next they set out to find a tailor specializing in military uniforms. Measurements were taken and put on file until orders were received giving them their assigned branches of the Army. Two days of visiting acquaintances proved too short to make the rounds they had hoped for. A final embrace and each headed his own way. Rufus boarded a sailing ship for Boston to catch up with his family. Fred was off to Virginia to visit relatives before traveling to his home near St. Louis. Ulysses once again would pass through Philadelphia, Harrisburg, Pittsburgh, and down the Ohio River stopping at whichever ports attracted the steamboat. Sly Bob Hazlitt, king of pranksters and a fellow Buckeye, planned to accompany Lyss as far as Marietta, Ohio.

He did no sightseeing, no visiting on his homeward journey. His travels brought relief from the regimen of the Academy. Yet there was new apprehension at the unknown. The primary unknown thing was where he would be placed by the Army. Graduates had been given the opportunity to request first and second choices. He listed Cavalry, formally listed as "Dragoons" by the Army, on top, though he knew his chances were not great. Top ranking students typically selected Engineers, Cavalry, or Artillery. Selections were normally filled by class rank from the top regardless of ability for duty. Lyss was twenty-first out of thirty-nine, or rather twenty-first out of ninety-six by Grandma Simpson's calculation, but he felt he must list Cavalry anyway. And it was no secret that the Cavalry was being diminished on orders from

Washington.

As second choice he listed Fourth Infantry. This choice would be to a regiment that was currently growing, thus creating opportunities for advancement. The number of officers of each and every grade was strictly limited by Congress. Advancement could only be had by the death or resignation of officers of the same rank (or higher causing a chain of promotions) or during a time of build-up. He knew also that the Fourth Infantry could be sent anywhere giving officers the opportunity to see various regions of the country.

Ulysses and Bob secured passage at a special military rate on a large comfortable sidewheel paddleboat that was scheduled through from Pittsburgh to Louisville with advertised stops only at Wheeling, Marietta, and Cincinnati. The river level was perfect for steaming. The crew was efficient and the boat was in top condition. Less than half the cabins were filled and one was filled by Lyss. Each time he opened his cabin door, he felt that he had been promoted to "gentleman." The only excitement for Lyss was when they pulled out of Marietta. They were just clearing the mouth of the Muskingum River when they met the inbound *Clarion*. Lyss strained to catch a glimpse of Patrick or Tevia or Captain Hendricks. For a fleeting moment the two boats passed. The opportunity quickly passed with it. He did not know if his friends were still aboard the *Clarion*. Rivermen changed frequently, but these three were unusually loyal to their boat.

Passing by familiar scenes evoked past experiences

at Maysville, Ripley, Higginsport, and Augusta. The large craft moored at night above a huge left bend before steaming into Cincinnati with the sun's morning rays. With his feet firmly on the Cincinnati Landing he headed directly to Parker's Livery where he reckoned to catch a ride to Bethel. He was soon riding with an Irish teamster, a tiny fellow, who piled one adventurous story atop another from the beginning of the trip to the end.

Ulysses was well aware that Lucy King would not be waiting for him in White Oak Creek Canyon. Nor would she be waiting anywhere else for that matter. She had enjoyed a lovely Christmas wedding and was living in an upstairs apartment in Batavia. The familiar sights on his homeward journey were comforting, though not as enchanting as two years previous. The Grant home in Bethel was not the home of his childhood.

Once again his father had purchased a young saddle horse, this time a permanent gift. It had a beautiful brown coat with flowing mane and tale. It had a peculiar aloofness, a persnickety attitude. He was so stylish that Lyss named him "Fashion."

Upon visiting the neighborhoods of Georgetown, he found that chums from earlier days were all busy making a living. They had little time to spare. On afternoons when he was in Georgetown he joined Mrs. Bailey for tea. She insisted that the Doctor and she hold a reception at their home in his honor. A formal affair was held with all the leading citizens attending. Fred Dent had taken a detour from his homeward journey and stayed with Lyss for three days. Fortunately he was available to accompany Lyss to the Bailey fete.

A good portion of the summer was happily spent on the Simpson farm. He helped Uncle Samuel make hay and shock wheat. He repaired harness and tended livestock. He made the rounds to all the local horse auctions.

Jesse Grant was busy managing his expanding business interests. Upon moving to Bethel two years earlier he had gone into partnership with Mr. Eli A. Collins, the man he purchased the tannery from. Jesse worked the tannery while Collins established a leather wholesale store in Galena, Illinois. There Collins also purchased hides and pelts to be shipped to Bethel. Lyss' brother Simpson moved to Galena to be a clerk at the store. The prospering community was fast becoming the jumping off point for the upper reaches of the Mississippi river.

Orders arrived near the end of July: "2LT Ulysses S. Grant; You are hereby ordered to report to Fourth Infantry, Jefferson Barracks, Missouri on or by the thirtieth day of September." Lyss saw to it that the next outbound mail carried instructions to the New York tailor to prepare and forward the infantry uniform. His official oath was sworn before the Bethel justice of the peace. Required documents were promptly completed and sent to Washington City.

Uncertainties were expelled from his mind. Vague ideas congealed into a plan of action. He confirmed to himself that when the time came he would be ready. He would welcome a new chapter in his life: a new beginning; new surroundings; new experiences. He would be up to whatsoever tasks he was given. He started reading St. Louis newspapers and searched out what information he could about the region.

One morning he visited the family of Thomas Hamer. Hamer was absent on business for the district court. Lyss informed the family of his assigned duty station and requested Mrs. Hamer to convey his thanks for appointment to the Academy. The same afternoon he caught Thomas Morris at home. He was amazed at the breadth of knowledge expounded by the former senator. After multitudinous diversified topics were covered, the discussion centered upon the Republic of Texas.

"I want you to be aware that there is a conspiracy about," Tom Morris instructed, "by my senate friends from the South to bring Texas into the Union for their own benefit. Not that Texas wouldn't be a good fit in its own right. These gentlemen want Texas to tip the balance in Congress to their favor. They're proposing a condition of admission to be included that the Republic may be divided into up to five individual states after admission." He leaned back into his stuffed leather chair and held up fingers: two then four then six then eight then ten. "Five states make ten senators – ten! As new states are brought forth out of the prairie frontier beyond the Mississippi River, these men will hold them for ransom until they get a new state of their own. Slavery should have suffered a slow lingering death by now. It no longer sustains itself across Virginia and Maryland nor across Kentucky and Tennessee. Only the advent of sugar and cotton farther south has resurrected the institution. The whole sad mess is propped up by a powerful few proponents! That and tradition! I dare say that plantations could be operated at better economy with hired workers, but everyone's afraid to try it. The way it is, the Upper South has an enticing market for their unnecessary slaves. We are caught in a revolving wheel. No one knows how to apply the brake and stop it from turning. As I was saying, these gentlemen see Texas as a ready-made answer to any rightful territory that applies for statehood.

"There will be unrelenting pressure until Texas is admitted into the Union. It is inevitable that it be so. Keep in mind that England has made serious overtures to the Texans. France and Spain have done the same to some degree, also. This we must keep in check. Mexico has not divorced herself from the region and still disputes the legitimacy of the Republic of Texas. So, as inevitable as it may be, it will not be an easy thing."

Tom Morris leaned forward with his face close to Lyss. With a practiced stern glare he drove home his final point to the young officer, "West Point teaches you the art and science of being a military man. This you have learned and I trust that you will do well in it. What they do not teach you is that politics directs the Army and the Navy. This is as it should be in a republic such as ours. It is a good deal from perfect." He used the orator's voice that he usually reserved for the Senate floor, "There will be times, Ulysses, that you will need to trust in your heart that in the end our form of government will prevail for good!"

Ulysses' new uniform and sword arrived in splendid condition. He could not have been more satisfied. The next morning he headed for Georgetown to meet and greet everyone he knew. Upon returning to Bethel he witnessed an acquaintance, a stable hand at the stage station across the street, wearing a mock uniform. The man was strutting back and forth barking orders to a straw man to the delight of gathered bystanders. The ridicule was not lost on Ulysses. He put aside his uniform until his departure for the West.

When the day of departure came, Fashion was tied to the rear of the carriage. Uncle Samuel Simpson drove his mother and nephew to Cincinnati. They had had a fine dinner at P. O'Rourke's Cafe on Third Street. Lyss bought a novel at a bookstore two doors down, then off to the Landing they went. Uncle and Grandmother stood watch over Ulysses' single trunk, saddle, and horse while he made arrangements for passage. He booked a stateroom on the *Tigress,* a midsized sternwheeler bound for St. Louis. He stayed onboard for the night and stood on deck in the morning when the vessel shoved-off.

The *Tigress* disregarded the river towns that Ulysses had visited on his first trip downriver. The boat ran night as well as day to hurry passengers to their destinations. Louisville was their first port, a quick overnight stop. Pulling out in the morning they immediately entered the Portland Canal which provided a bypass of the Falls of the Ohio. A sense of adventure was rekindled in Lyss as the *Tigress* slipped through the locks that as a boy he had only seen from the bank. The remainder of the trip would be through undiscovered territory for him.

Grandma Simpson had reminded Lyss that from Pittsburgh to Louisville he was retracing the journey begun by Meriwether Lewis forty years earlier. Immediately below the Falls of the Ohio, across on the Indiana side at the cabin of George Rogers Clark, Lewis was joined by William Clark. From here the two men commenced their stunning journey together to the Pacific. Though Ulysses was traveling effortlessly and in comfort, he nonetheless felt a kinship with the two famous Captains of the U.S. Army. Down the length of the Ohio River and up the Mississippi River to St. Louis, he would closely observe each bend and each hill as he passed. Perhaps this would be the beginning of his own historic pilgrimage.

Jefferson Barracks

Two riders headed north by west from Jefferson Barracks into vibrant fall foliage. James "Pete" Longstreet was tall and lean with dark complexion and wavy black hair. He had a princely look in the saddle. Ulysses "Sam" Grant was shorter with pale ruddy skin and sandy-reddish hair. Only his uniform and sword kept him from being taken as a millwright's apprentice or perhaps a cooper. Pete was talkative and gregarious. Ulysses was quiet and excessively shy. They seemed to be an odd pair to throw in together. Yet here they were, off on a common quest, anxious to accomplish their destination only a short distance from their appointed station.

Pete Longstreet led the way. He knew the route well as he had ridden it many times. Lyss did not mind following his friend. Pete had preceded him to Jefferson Barracks by one year and knew the ins and outs of the place and its surroundings. Lyss had been there only thirty days and was absorbing all he could to make his way. Pete took the unassuming fledgling officer under his wing much like he had done at the Academy. Where others saw a backward dull unimaginative country boy he saw a conscientious meticulous tried-and-true lad who surmounted every obstacle. He secretly envied Lyss' mathematical genius and superb horsemanship hidden within his quiet unflappable manner.

Jefferson Barracks was the largest military post in the country. Its seventeen-hundred acres reached westward two miles from the bank of the Mississippi River. Drills and maneuvers for all branches of the army were conducted upon its expansive rolling hills. Infantry, artillery, and cavalry each trained in small groups and large, independently and in unison. It was no secret that a build-up was in process to address two concerns of the United States in the west: the Indian question and the Texas question.

Grant had been attached to a company containing only thirty-six privates. All companies were woefully shorthanded. New enlistees were being added regularly. Officers were generally in short supply. Even so, Colonel Steven Kearney, perhaps sensing impending deployment, permitted many and frequent leaves of absence for officers of all classifications. Captains and Lieutenants were constantly shifted about to fill gaps. Junior officers did duties normally reserved for senior officers. Within a month of arrival Lieutenant Grant was in temporary command of his company, giving orders as though he were Captain.

Pete and Ulysses shared a particular common bond: an abiding friendship with Fred Dent. A junior

Lieutenant the same as them, Fred had been assigned to the Sixth Infantry. He was expected to leave this day for Fort Towson on the western frontier. Lyss had promised to visit his former roommate and meet his family. White Haven, Fred's home, was only five miles away. Special duties for all officers of the Fourth Infantry had delayed their little journey for five days. They feared they may have little time to see their friend off. Lyss could not know that Pete had an additional ulterior motive.

With no opportunities for gallivanting until now, Ulysses yearned for the mysteries of the deep woods. He longed to see the fertile fields and singing brooks Fred had told him about. He was curious to see how a plantation operated. A home-cooked meal would be welcomed, too. They cleared the military reserve and headed up a narrow wagon road. They pulled off to the side to let a light wagon pulled by a single horse pass.

A grey-haired slave stopped his wagon, "Hayda', sirs! Y'all want tu' pick out a melon for your own? Theys all belongs tu' the army anyways. Help yourselves!"

The driver turned and hefted a fat green striped melon. Pete tipped his hat slightly and nudged his knee against his horse to move past the wagon.

Lyss acknowledged the offer, "Mighty tempting, but no. We need to keep moving." He caught up alongside Longstreet. "I can't tell you how great it is to be back in the saddle. My boys have kept me so tied down that I'm afraid Fashion here has not gotten his proper attention. He needs the exercise and I need to be free from drills. Actually I should say that in the singular; it's been one continuous drill from the day I arrived."

Pete smiled, "Imagine how the men of your company feel!"

Lyss, "You're right. They have become surly and some of that has rubbed off on me."

Pete, "Lesson number one: officers need to keep independent from their men. Keep guard that you are responding to your own dictates and not the whims of the men." Actually, Pete had given quite a few "lesson number ones."

Lyss inquired, "I've often wondered. Fred Dent often has called you 'cousin'. How does that fit?"

Pete explained, "My mother was a Dent. She and Fred's father had the same grandparents when they were back in Virginia. Of course that's still the case although their grandparents and parents are gone. Fred's mother grew up in the Virginia homeland, also. Everyone likes Mrs. Dent and so will you. A gentle and kind woman, she is. To let you in on a secret, I surmise that she longs to be back in Virginia or Maryland in civilized society. Now the Colonel, he's a different sort. Most find Colonel Dent to be feisty to the degree of cantankerous. He views the world as it was fifty years ago. Modern ways are an affront to his being."

Lyss asked, "Is 'Colonel' a courtesy title or did he earn it by service?"

Pete elaborated, "No military service. The Colonel, originally out of Maryland, sees himself as a gentleman farmer. He bought an old Spanish land grant and moved out of Saint Louis to partially retire. He had done rightly well for himself in business, first in Pittsburgh then later here in Saint Louis. He merchandised in goods for the Indian trade. Back then he was one of the first to own his own steamboat to move his goods, so they say. He mixed with the top people during territorial days. Since statehood his old group has gradually been on the wane."

Longstreet interrupted himself to point out a grove of sycamores that marked their turn-off. A narrow path to the right would save considerable distance from the roundabout lane route.

Pete picked up where he left off concerning Colonel Dent, "The Colonel and his wife Ellen love to entertain. They hold lavish garden parties and balls. Anyone from the old guard in the city is welcome to come and stay in the country for a few days. I think the plantation life is sustained just to keep Ellen happy. The Colonel takes undue pride in experimental livestock. It appears to me to be more show than sound economy. None of his sons, including Fred, have much of an interest in the workings of agriculture."

Riding down into a ravine and crossing a brook, Lyss questioned, "Does this stream have a name?"

Pete, "Why yes, it's Gravois Creek. You've often heard Fred speak of it."

Yes, Lyss had heard Fred speak of the Gravois. But he had conjured something much larger, something akin to White Oak Creek back in Ohio.

Pete continued, "Anyway, don't let the Colonel's gruff crust throw you. He barks as loud as a coon dog, but underneath is a puppy wanting to be scratched behind the ears." Pete had a purpose in having Lyss understand the Colonel. "After you are acquainted, you will find a caring and generous man."

The path gradually widened to wagon tracks. They rode past a fenced sheep pasture, then on past small patches of hay and wheat stubble. A gang of four slaves was shocking corn stalks on the far side of a field. A granary of hewn logs sat empty along the way. They approached a neat though modest cabin. To the side, a young man was tugging at the lever of a cider press.

Pete hailed, "Yo, John! Look what I brought with me. This is Sam Grant, Fred's roommate at the Academy. Sam, you've heard Fred talk about his no good oldest brother John, right?"

John returned the banter, "And to think that we were doing quite fine out here in the wilderness until the Army saw fit to send the likes of you out here from the Atlantic."

Pete dismounted and Ulysses did likewise. Pete and John embraced. John gave Lyss' hand a vigorous shake.

Pete, "John, we shall not tarry. We hope to catch Fred before he heads off to the hinterlands."

John informed the two riders, "I saw Fred on Sunday. He planned to leave yesterday for Saint Charles. He was to tag along with supply wagons headed to Fort Gibson on the Arkansas River. From there he expected to find an escort through the Indian Territory to Fort Towson down by the Red River. I don't know if he actually left or not." He handed Pete a jug, "Here, take some fresh sweet cider to the Old Man – first fruits as it were. Move along; I won't keep you!"

Second Lieutenant Ulysses S. Grant discovered White Haven to be somewhat less than the palace that Fred had told about. There were no monumental Greek columns, no granite façade. What he found was a large sturdy comfortable well kept, though a bit aged, family home. He immediately saw why so many fellow officers came to visit. It had an inviting, relaxed appeal.

Resting upon a small knoll a ways back from Gravois Creek that traversed the farm, the rectangular two-story house was covered with clapboard siding. Square wooden columns supported a porch with a roofed second-floor balcony. Simple tasteful ornamentation trimmed the structure. Honeysuckle draped itself on wide and tall stone chimneys at each end. A foundation that exposed itself as it reached down the slope was also well laid with local limestone. A single-story addition to the left blended with the original structure.

A robust woman servant looked up from sweeping leaves from the porch. She stepped to the end of the porch and called to children playing in the orchard, "Boys! You young 'uns git over here and take these horses 'round back." She turned to the visitors. "Sakes alive if it hain't Mars James come for a visit! Colonel Dent is inside, jes' sittin' in his easy chair reading his newspaper. Let me put down this broom and I'll take y'all right in. The Colonel always enjoys your visits. He'll be glad to meet your friend here. I'll tell Mary to put on extra for supper."

Pete scolded, "Not so fast, Rose. You take this jug in while we clean our boots. No sense in making extra work for you."

Rose caught herself, "Oh, dear me! You've come to see young Fred off! Oh, dear! I'm afraid he left early yesterday – left before the rooster crowed! Of course you're welcome anyways. Should I make up beds for tonight?"

A string of children rounded the corner of the house. They were led by a small girl with tussled brown hair and a mussed plain dress. She held a tattered bird's nest in each hand. She stood beside the porch steps and stared up at Ulysses with her mouth agape.

Pete spoke teasingly, "What's the matter, Emma? Won't you say 'good day' to Sam?"

A slave lad showed Rose another gathered nest, "We've been collecting nests for Emma, see?"

Rose commanded, "Yes, yes, I see. You boys tend to the horses." She directed her stare at the little girl, "Young lady, I will see you upstairs!"

The Colonel was sitting in a wicker chair with large cushions, his feet on a wooden stool in front of a warm fireplace. A side table was piled high with assorted books, journals, and ledgers. A small opened trunk was stuffed with newspapers. Beside his chair was a small stand with a rack of pipes and tobacco. Ulysses was struck by the man's stout frame and big round head with frumpy shocks of hair that apparently did not respond well to a brush. Lyss surmised that the Colonel may have recently stepped out of a Dickens novel.

Longstreet made the formal introductions.

The Colonel burst forth, "So you're Honest Sam Grant! Let me get a look at you!" He nodded approvingly, "I congratulate you on the completion of your studies at West Point. I have it on authority from my son, and from Cousin Pete here, that you are a first rate fellow. I wish to thank you for helping my son make the grade!"

Ulysses was taken aback, "I feel that you have been misinformed, sir. Fred is his own man."

The Colonel chided, "No need for modesty. I know my son. Now I insist that you two stay for supper." He turned to Rose, "Tell Mary we'll have mutton with sweet potatoes. What do you boys say to apricot pie? Yes, that will do."

He waved his house servant away and fingered an unlit pipe. He laid his newspaper on the floor beside his chair. "Now let me see if I have this right," he mused. "You're the champion horseman. You're the one who never reads his texts a second time and who sets down original solutions to mathematical problems, is that about right?"

Ulysses did not know how to respond. Pete quietly grinned and nodded in the positive.

The Colonel went on, "Let me see, you were president of the literary society. At the same time you shared the title of head prankster along with my son. Seems that you had to extricate him on more than one occasion."

Lyss' face was turning red. He wondered what exaggerations Fred had been telling. Pete let out a laugh.

The Colonel changed the topic, "I understand that you grew up with a plow in your hand." He went on to describe his plantation, its crops and buildings. He delved into details about experiments with grain varieties and exotic livestock. He told how he was an early adopter of improved farm machinery. He damned Whigs and Yankees for upsetting the apple cart for merchants such as himself.

Two young girls kept peeking through the open door into the reading room. They jostled for position to get a look at Ulysses, giggling and running away. Finally father called them in to be introduced. Emma, now with washed hands, brushed hair, and a clean yellow dress, would soon turn seven. Nellie was a young fifteen. They stood erect and smiled with grins, but did not speak. Once back through the door they again broke out with giggles then ran upstairs.

Pete chimed in, "And Miss Julia, will she be presented this day?"

Colonel Dent, "Why no! Don't you know? She is now off to spend the winter season with Carrie O'Fallon! They came for her on Sunday."

Ellen Dent joined the family and guests at supper. Lyss found her to be exceedingly polite, quite gracious, yet unassuming. She was small with delicate features; some would consider her to be on the frail side. She was a devout Methodist the same as Lyss' mother. Yet she covered her head with a small fragile kerchief rather than his mother's bonnet.

Ellen Dent asked her guests, "Did you see Emma's birds' nest collection today?"

Pete scoured his memory but came up blank.

Lyss commented, "Yes indeed! And quite a gathering expedition it must have been." He smiled at the beaming girl, then turned back to Mrs. Dent. "Let's see, the children had three robin's nests, one goldfinch, one delicate bluebird, and one that must be either cardinal or blue jay. Those are the ones I saw, anyway."

Ellen asked, "And how do you know one from another?"

Lyss addressed Emma, "Each variety of bird has a peculiar way of forming its nest. Some in a tree, some on the ground, some with grass or mud or twigs."

Ellen concurred, "Yes, it's a natural thing that the Good Lord instilled in them before they gasped their first breath. Now tell me, are any two robins' nests entirely alike?"

Lyss, "No, no, I suppose not. Each and every one that there ever was made was put together in its own manner."

Ellen smiled approvingly, "Every little thing of nature is unique. The Lord nurtured the soil and let a seed fall into it. He brought the rain and the seed sprouted. The sprout bathed itself in sunshine and grew tall and strong. It put forth blossoms and produced fruit to attract insects and birds. Birds built their nests in notches of the branches. The trunk and limbs put on heavy bark so that children could climb and discover nests."

Lyss was intrigued. Pete enjoyed a bite of mutton.

Ellen continued with her parable, "When a child climbs a tree and reaches for a nest, her length and her weight place her in touch with the bark of a tree in a way such that no other person will ever experience. As she reaches for the nest, the sun and clouds and wind and leaves form light and shadows that no other person will exactly experience. In that moment the Lord has created an experience that will never be duplicated for any other person."

Lyss nodded approvingly. The Colonel passed a faint smile to his wife.

Ellen shared, "I want all of my children to experience nature. I want them to squish their toes in the mud. I want their feet to feel the cool pebbles in the bottoms of brooks. I want them to hear the wind in the pines and the buzz of bumble bees. It is then that they know that the Lord has looked down and arranged his creation to bring special moments just for them. I'm afraid as adults we forget to savor these moments. Every time we take on a responsibility we push aside our childhood instincts. We fail to relish what God has given us. I have seen it in our Fred when he arrived home from West Point. You young officers would do well to step back and reflect from time to time."

Over pie, the Colonel reminisced about earlier days. He told about bringing Ellen and little John and all his belongings and trade wares down the Ohio River on a raft made up of three flatboats chained together. They trekked across the tip of Illinois and crossed into what was then Upper Louisiana Territory. He first set up shop in Saint Charles and traded up into the frontier along the Missouri River. Later he built a waterfront warehouse in Saint Louis and settled his family in the growing town. He easily dropped names of associates who were leading citizens of early Saint Louis. Both William Clark, governor of the territory, and the first governor after statehood, Alexander McNair, had sat in the chair now occupied by Ulysses.

The two young officers from Jefferson Barracks stayed the night. They had an early breakfast. Mary made it a feast to be remembered.

Colonel Dent was on the porch to see them off, "I always enjoy your company, Pete. Now Sam, you feel free to stop by whenever you so choose. One day we'll ride my fields and you can get a look at my stock. I would especially value your opinion of my horses. Now remember, if you get the slightest word about Fred inform me immediately."

The two young officers headed back to their duties at Jefferson Barracks.

Pete opined, "It appears that you hit it off well with the Old Man. I've never seen him warm up to anyone so quickly." He added with a laugh, "Especially a Yankee such as yourself!" In an earnest tone he added, "More importantly, Ellen Dent took a shine to you. As I said, she usually gets what she wants."

Pete spent the remainder of their ride telling Ulysses about the missing daughter.

"Julia is now seventeen." "She spent the past winter at a finishing school in the city and had been at White Haven for the summer." "The O'Fallons, where she will spend the winter, are the top family on everyone's social list." "Julia has never met an animal that she didn't fall in love with whether dog, cat, bird, raccoon, or frog." "She sings and dances with the best of them." "She loves to walk the woods and wade the streams." "There isn't a horse too fast for her."

Young Ulysses slowly caught on to Pete Longstreet's theme. It would not hurt to look into the matter if the situation presented itself. For now, he had a profession to master.

White Haven

"No, Lyss, I will not marry you. I just am not ready for such things."

It was an honest and true answer. Julia Dent and young Ulysses had known each other for only three months.

Well before they met, winter had settled in at Jefferson Barracks. Blustery cold days with whistling wind and spitting snow had been interspersed with those of tranquil sunshine. The daily routine of the military post on the bluff above the Mississippi River had continued without alteration. Continually arriving recruits were from time to time formed into new companies for the Third Infantry as well as the Fourth Infantry. The sounds of drum cadences were frequently mixed with the rattle of building construction.

Colonel Kearney kept the post operating at optimal performance. Everything was as it should be – nothing out of place, no one out of line. Although he maintained the highest expectations from his officers, they were permitted to follow their fancy when not conducting drills or performing necessary duties. Most officers frequented Saint Louis and many took leave for farther destinations

Lieutenant Ulysses Grant often amused himself by reading on a knoll overlooking the river. He would look up from his book at a steamboat passing below all by its lonesome. He would wonder about its passengers and their destinations. He hoped to one day travel the river all the way down to New Orleans. His thoughts drifted back to his first steamboat trip: Captain Hendricks, Patrick, Tevia, and yes to Ellie and Ida, and even LeMunyon.

He began an earnest study of mathematics texts that he had passed over lightly at West Point. Early on, he had written to Professor William Church, mathematics instructor at the Academy, requesting an appointment as Professor's Assistant when a vacancy occurred. He had received an encouraging response. On wintry days when snow drifts took the sharp edges off the military post and muffled the sounds of its bustle, young Ulysses buried his mind in his texts. Hours of concentration made him oblivious to snow sifting in at his window sill.

Ulysses got along well with all of the lieutenants and most of the captains. He gradually realized that others of his rank were coming to him for advice on how to handle their units. Captains were giving him preferential treatment. These he took as signs that he was performing appropriately, perhaps exemplary.

Weekly visits to White Haven were his most

welcomed respite. The Dents made him feel at home with their family. Perhaps he was a surrogate for their son who was serving at his designated post far off in the Indian Territory. Anyway, Lyss found that wonderful meals and gentle conversations at White Haven were good tonic for a military man. He began scrounging discarded newspapers from fellow officers. These he would carry to Colonel Dent offering news from cities around the country. He found that he could tactfully debate current events and politics with the elder gentleman without raising the man's ire to dangerous limits.

Wherever he went, whatever he did around the plantation grounds, Emma followed. The only way to slip away was to mount Fashion and ride away from the house. He soon found Nellie joining him for these jaunts. The Colonel did indeed have fine carriage horses and riding horses, many mixed with Arabian blood. The work horses were of basic stock. Occasionally he would fish with Fred's younger brother Lewis. Older brother John frequently invited him to hunt; always he politely declined.

Ulysses found that work cleared his mind. He began pitching in here and there along beside the slaves in their labors. He soon knew them all by name. Regularly Lyss would accompany Old Bob as he would drive a mule to the woods, hitch it to a felled log, and drag the timber up near the springhouse. There Lyss would help saw the trunk into lengths. Next would begin the eternal task of splitting chunks into firewood. Old Bob would sing an endless mournful meter as he swung his ax.

One day Ulysses asked, "Where does that song come from, Old Bob? I can't place it."

Old Bob thought a moment, "Don't rightly know. It's always been in my head as far as I can recollect. Must a' been born in me. The Good Lord put it in my soul, shore 'nuf."

The swinging of the ax continued. The song continued. Lyss used a wedge and a heavy hammer to split apart larger blocks.

Lyss asked, "How old are you, Old Bob? You swing that ax mighty well!"

Old Bob replied without glancing up, "Don't rightly know that, neither. I was given to the Colonel when he was a boy. So I reckon I would be older than him by some years."

Lyss continued questioning, "That was in Maryland? So, you came down the Ohio with the family?"

Old Bob placed the head of the ax on the ground and leaned on the handle. A far off look overtook him, "T'was jest me and the Colonel and Miss Ellen and little John. We cut loose at Pittsburgh and we drifted away on that wild river. On and on it flowed away from Maryland. More than twenty days we floated far away to the Illinois country. In them days boats only came down the river – no getting back."

Old Bob stood silently staring at his chopping block. Lyss longed to ask about the man's family back in Maryland, but dared not breach the topic. He positioned his wedge and gave it a whack.

Lyss broke the silence, "You and the Colonel must have had quite a few adventures here in Missouri."

Old Bob again took up his chopping, "Shore 'nuf. I reckon I know the Colonel better'n anyone. I don't want to talk about it now."

The woodchopper took up his song. His singing was slower than before. He sang with a deeper voice. Music seldom had an effect upon Ulysses one way or another. However, the exaggerated woefulness that he now heard reached deep into his marrow.

On a mild day of February, 1844, Julia Dent stepped out of a large fancy carriage in front of White Haven. In doing so, the girl of eighteen was stepping out of her whirlwind society affairs and back into her childhood. She was ready to leave the weddings and parties behind. She longed for simpler familiar surroundings.

On the third day after she settled in, Ulysses made his weekly visit to White Haven. Julia was not surprised to have a young officer call. It was a commonplace event at White Haven. Anxious to go for a ride through the country and needing a companion, she invited Lyss to accompany her. He accepted. Together they rode slowly off through hay fields and woods to the back of the farm. There they took a little road towards the crossroads hamlet of Afton where Julia wished to mail a letter.

Julia broke the silence, "Papa says that you have become a regular at our modest home."

Lyss replied, "Your family has been most gracious. It's like I packed up my home and brought it with me to Jefferson Barracks. It's a wonderful contrast to being on a military post."

He could have added that his headache spells ceased once he began visiting the little plantation.

Julia shared, "Fred never told me much about his days at West Point. I think that he was in constant apprehension about the possibility of being sent home. Now he's off to the frontier and heaven knows when I will see him again. Cousin Pete tells me you and Fred were tight friends at school."

"We hit it off right away, just like we knew each other all along," Lyss agreed. He ventured, "I hope it will be the same with you and me."

Julia gave an innocent smile, "Why not? I'm sure it will be." She added with a tease, "In my short time at home I have discovered that both of my little sisters are in love with you."

During the remainder of the ride to Afton, Lyss answered Julia's questions about Fred and West Point. On the return trip she asked about Lyss' horse. That opened a long discourse on horses in general.

"This is Psyche. Mostly Arabian," she said proudly. "Papa gave her to me last summer when I got home from school. Something of a graduation present you could say."

She turned off the road onto a path that led cross-country. She quickened the pace. Lyss caught up. Again she sped ahead. Lyss responded accordingly. Soon they were flying across a meadow at break-neck speed. Although Lyss had ridden this path once in the fall season, he found that he had to concentrate to keep abreast. No doubt about it! Pete was right! This girl could ride! Right then and there, in the midst of leaping over a brook, young Ulysses was smitten.

Julia eased up a little as they approached the summit of a rounded hill. Still, she kept a quick pace, looking neither left nor right until they approached the split-rail fence surrounding the house and accompanying outbuildings. She came to a quick stop at the side gate. She leapt off and stroked Psyche's hindquarters. She walked her chestnut horse through the gate towards the stable barn.

Without looking up she said to her riding companion, "Well, here we are. Thank you for helping Psyche to get a work-out. That little jaunt is just what she needed."

Lyss offered, "Fashion here is underworked himself. We should exercise them together again soon."

The young officer lingered at White Haven as long as he dared without finding trouble later at the barracks. He rode out to White Haven the following day just as soon as he could break away. His visits became so frequent that everyone soon knew what his business was about. Everyone except Julia, that is. She simply enjoyed his companionship.

They rode long rides around the countryside. They took long walks in the woods. They shared a harmony with the natural world. They quickly discovered that they had read the same novels and poets. He listened to her sing. Others said she had a talent for it. He couldn't really tell. Singing was her only artistic endeavor. She neither drew nor worked with needles nor dallied about the kitchen.

In the early springtime Ulysses escorted Julia to balls at Jefferson Barracks and in the city. She would dance with her many acquaintances; he would watch. It occurred to him that she exhibited features of both belles he had encountered on the Ohio River, Ida and Ellie. At the plantation she was Ida: warm; caring; quick to smile; and easygoing. At a party she was a socialite, something like Ellie chatting a flutter of nonsense, yet kinder and more genteel.

Julia, like Kate, had acquired the finer traits that were indoctrinated at finishing school. Her conversation was easy and bright. She did not have the beauty that Kate possessed. Yet she had a charm that sprung from wide innocence. Like Lucy, she immediately loved every animal she met. Whether tame or wild, gentle or vicious, she gave each the same kindness. Unlike Lucy, she never let practical things steal her pleasures.

An event on one April day solidified Julia's estimation of Lyss' character. Upon arriving for one of his visits he found her saddened by the death of her pet canary. She had wrapped the poor bird in a dainty kerchief, placed it back into its cage, and hung the covered cage in an alcove on the back porch. Ulysses instructed her to leave it there until the next day. Upon the return of her uniformed companion he was accompanied by seven other officers. He had a little hand-made wooden coffin. No canary ever had a finer burial.

April brought an abrupt change to the routine at Jefferson Barracks. The entire Third Infantry was ordered to Fort Jesup in western Louisiana. Within days they packed up. Each man and every article was loaded aboard steamboats. The flotilla pushed off on the twentieth day of the month. Up above on the parade grounds cannon fired salutes. Those left behind saluted as the post band played. In a short while the last of the paddleboats was out of sight. South down the Mississippi they went. At the mouth of the Red River they turned west through bayou country and on up that river to Natchitoches. Above the old town at the frontier port of Grand Ecore they disembarked. Westward they marched to the vicinity of the Sabine River. There they made their camp. The unwritten but obvious intent was to be poised to squelch any troubles that may erupt across the border in the Republic of Texas.

Everyone at Jefferson Barracks expected that the Fourth Infantry would soon follow. Ulysses promptly applied for and received a leave of twenty days, effective May first, to visit his parents. He put his things in order at his quarters. He packed a single bag for the trip.

He awoke early on the day of departure. He made his rounds to bid farewell to his friends. Nervously he awaited the proper moment to head out. Before going to Saint Louis to catch a steamboat to Louisville or Cincinnati he had a mission to carry out. He directed Fashion onto the familiar route to White Haven.

At promptly ten o'clock Ulysses stepped onto the porch and tapped with the knocker. One of the house servants, Kitty, answered the door.

"Mornin', Master Grant," she said, "and a wonderful mornin' it 'tis. Miss Julia will be down shortly. She is expectin' y'all. Come on in and have a chair. Truth is, it's hard tellin' how long it'll be waitin' for that girl to preen up."

"Thank you, Kitty," he replied, "but I'll wait out here on the porch." He did not mention that he wished to avoid Colonel Dent this morning.

He sat awhile, then he stood. He paced to and fro. He fidgeted with his cap. He turned his class ring. Julia sprung from the doorway fresh and lively.

"Cleopatra had kittens, new this morning!" Julia beamed. "Do you want to come see them?"

Ulysses was not to be distracted, "Maybe later. I don't have much time. Let's walk in the orchard."

He guided her to the springtime orchard bursting with blossoms. All was going according to his plan. He held her hand. This he had never done. Their fingers intertwined. She allowed their arms to swing together as they walked. Smatterings of sunlight and shadow filtered through the overhead branches as they strolled the orchard path. They stopped on a cart bridge and listened to the brook below sing its rippled meter.

"So, you're off to Ohio," Julia stated the obvious. "Psyche and I will miss you and Fashion while you are away. I should mark the days until you return."

Lyss jumped at his opportunity, "The number of days may be more uncertain than we know."

Julia asked quizzically, "How so?"

Lyss explained, "If, by chance, the Fourth is deployed while I am on leave, and if orders reach me before my return, I may be instructed to report directly to the new post."

He looked into her eyes to see if she understood his meaning. She was obviously puzzled.

"Yes, I suppose so," she said hesitatingly.

Lyss took both of her hands. He felt a tingling sensation radiate from his hands up his arms and on throughout his being. He was apprehensive. Yet he pressed on.

"Julia," he got to the point, "I do not know when we will next see each other. Take my class ring, please! Wear it until we next meet."

"No, Lyss, I will not marry you. I just am not ready for such things," she protested. "You told me once that if you ever gave your ring, it would be as an engagement. I'm not ready for that." She turned away, then turned back with hope in her eyes. "You are my best friend. The best that I have ever had! Please understand!"

Ulysses spent an agonizing ride to the Saint Louis Landing. Had he poorly handled what he had hoped to be a memorable experience? Julia had participated in weddings of some of her classmates; why wasn't she ready to be engaged? Was she afraid of what the Colonel would say? Yes, there was no doubt but that she was daddy's girl. An army officer's pay may do temporarily for the Colonel's son, but would it suffice for the husband of his eldest daughter? Could a fledgling officer muster the wherewithal to provide his little girl with the comforts to which she was entitled?

On the Landing, having procured passage through to Cincinnati, he was approached by a sergeant.

The soldier walked up to him and saluted, "Are you Lieutenant Grant?"

Lyss replied, "Yes, sir. I am Ulysses Grant."

Soldier, "Sir, I have a dispatch from the post."

Ulysses received the folded sealed paper and dismissed the sergeant. He presumed that his leave had been cancelled. However, it was a personal note from his friend Lieutenant Hazlitt. The note informed him that the Fourth Infantry had indeed been deployed to Fort Jesup to link up with the Third. Hazlitt pledged to oversee the transport of Lyss' trunk. His former classmate also suggested that Lyss continue his journey home while trying to avoid receiving orders until reporting back to Jefferson Barracks.

Lyss pondered this turn of events. Should he continue under his present orders? Or should he return to his company? He needed some time away from the Army. Perhaps away from Missouri he could think more clearly. He found himself wondering which choice Dan Ammen would make. His boyhood friend was always so level-headed, seemingly confident in every decision. He chose to follow Hazlitt's recommendation.

His passage back to Cincinnati somehow lacked the usual charm. He was listless. He could not concentrate on a book or on a card game. He wandered aimlessly about the decks taking note of neither passengers nor scenery. In order to lift his spirits he tried recalling each of his previous river experiences. All for naught; all thoughts ran back to Julia.

Arriving back at Bethel he filled each day he could with toil on the Simpson farm. He worked in the orchard; he worked in the hay fields; he mended fences and cleaned barns. He was well aware that when he would soon leave for the western borderlands there would be no way of knowing when he would see Ohio again. The American display of force may settle the Texas question quietly, or just as likely it may goad Mexico into a call to arms. There certainly was a popular national cry to thrust the western border of the country across Mexican held lands.

His labor cleared his mind of all troubling thoughts except one. How should he go about telling his father and mother that when he next returns he may be married? How should he tell them that his intended wife is accustomed to life on a plantation with an air of Southern aristocracy including slaves in the field and slaves in the house? Each day he devised a plan only to reject it by day's end. Perhaps it would be just as well to leave this one chore undone. Conversations with his father centered upon the elder's earlier travels from New Orleans to Texas with a stopover at Fort Jesup.

Julia decided she would make a formal gesture of marking the twenty days. In the hush of the still evening of the fifteenth day a queasy feeling overcame her. On day sixteen the sensation grew. By day seventeen she had no doubt as to its cause. She longed to see Ulysses. She knew that his regiment had taken off down the

Mississippi River. She was anxious that orders may have already sent him away from her. The next two days she sat on the porch watching for him. He did not come. On the twentieth day she rode Psyche slowly down the trail towards Jefferson Barracks. She stopped short of the buildings. She waited. She watched. She ached. Finally she turned her horse around and headed home. A tremendous cloudburst drenched her during the final leg of her trip.

Ellen Dent had seen to it that Julia's bedroom was remodeled. She transformed it from a girl's room to that of a young lady. New furniture was being taken upstairs when Julia returned from her ride. Mrs. Dent was disappointed in her daughter's lack of enthusiasm.

Sleeping in her new bed for the first time, Julia had a vivid dream about Ulysses. In her dream Ulysses arrived at noon in civilian clothes. She heard him telling her, "I will stay a week." In the morning she hurried to Nellie's room. There she told her sister about the dream and how real it all seemed.

Nellie chided, "Ha! That's one of your premonitions that can't possibly come true! His leave is expired and he is gone!"

Julia reluctantly agreed. She was prone to premonitions. She had learned to trust them. This one could not possibly happen as it appeared. Perhaps she needed to interpret its meaning. Perhaps she had secretly willed the dream to happen. She sat in her room reading poetry, looking for a hint of inspiration. None came.

At noon there was a commotion downstairs. Kitty

ran in from the porch with an air of excitement.

"Miss Julia! Miss Julia," she called. "Come quick! It's Mars John! Come quick! He has Lieutenant Grant with him! Miss Julia!"

It could not be! Was it a trick? She rushed down the steps. There he was! There he was in civilian clothes. There he was oddly disheveled in oversized farm chore clothes.

Nellie exclaimed, "It happened! It happened just like in Julia's dream!"

Julia did not care about the dream. She cared that Ulysses had come. But how did it happen to be?

Ulysses was sheepish at being presented to the family in his present condition. Still he wondered at Nellie's comment. Had Julia been dreaming about him?

John explained to the entire family about the clothes. Gravois Creek had turned into a raging torrent. Ulysses had forced his crossing, nearly being swept away and drowned. He had struggled up to John's cottage. John gave him nourishment and lent him clothes.

Ulysses explained that counter orders had never reached him. Upon returning at the expiration of his leave he found Lieutenant Richard Ewel in temporary command of the nearly deserted post. Lyss requested an extended leave for important business. Ewel sympathetically consented. Lyss would have one week free of duty, report to the barracks, and then ship out for Louisiana.

Julia knew that her father was wondering about what constituted "important business." She had her suspicions about what it meant.

Ellen Dent treated him like a returning hero. She invited, "The entire family is headed to Saint Louis for a wedding tomorrow. I'm afraid we failed to arrange an escort for Julia. Would you do the honors?"

Inclement weather continued into the morning. White Haven was a bustle of activity with everyone in the house being outfitted with their finery. The lady of the house and her daughters were radiant in their gay dresses. John was dapper. Ulysses, in newly cleaned and pressed uniform, sword at his side, struck a handsome form. The Colonel, in formal clothes from a bygone era, looked less stuffy than usual. Spruced up Kitty and Rose were likewise elegantly attired.

Fortunately, the weather broke during their early lunch. As they headed out the sky brightened. So did their spirits. The big carriage was tended by two men servants. It carried Ellen, the Colonel, and Emma as well as Kitty and Rose. Nellie chose to ride with John in his buggy. Lyss commandeered a second buggy for Julia and himself. The caravan got underway up the soggy road. Singing could be heard from one vehicle then from another as they made their way.

Ulysses had formulated a plan. His plan was to this time not follow a predetermined strategy. He would be alert to any opportunity that presented itself. Maybe a sentiment expressed at the wedding would be his cue. Perhaps on the way back home a comment about the happy couple would provide an opening.

The procession halted at a small bridge on a small

stream. At least the stream was usually small. This day the current was lapping over the deck. John and Lyss joined the carriage attendant who was inspecting the little structure. The three leaned and peered and studied from all angles. Soon they each nodded that all was safe to proceed.

John called to the driver, "All looks good! Come along!"

The driver proceeded ever so cautiously across the planks. Nellie shut her eyes while John hauled her and the attendant across. Lyss approached slowly, Julia at his side. She nervously eyed the trepid water.

Julia shifted nearer to Ulysses, "Our little buggy is so fragile! I will cling to you if you don't mind!"

She wrapped both arms around Lyss' right arm and squeezed tightly. Her head pressed against his shoulder. Lyss did not mind. Fate had given him an opportunity earlier than he imagined. But first, he needed to concentrate to ensure a successful crossing. He did not want a repeat of his Gravois Creek incident, especially with everyone ahead gazing back at his progress.

Once safely across he called to John and the coach driver, "All is well here!"

The procession resumed up a small slope. Julia still clung. Lyss drove his horse at a walk. The two front vehicles stretched ahead. Lyss watched for what he judged to be the proper degree of separation. He waited. The time was right! He stopped the buggy. Julia looked up at him.

This would be his one chance. He used the voice he

normally used for teasing Emma.

"Why, Miss Julia," he said, "How would you like to cling to me for the rest of your life?"

Julia did not hesitate, "Yes, Lyss. Yes I would!"

She kissed his cheek. He was thrilled. He wrapped the reins on a spindle. Right there on the little muddy road just past the little muddy creek, they embraced for the first time. They kissed for the first time. Whether real or imagined, a beam of sunshine shone down on them. It warmed Ulysses.

Julia was emboldened, "May I have your class ring?"

Ulysses fumbled with his gloves and ultimately presented her with his ring. She held it in her hand.

Julia stated, "I will accept this if you won't tell Papa that we are engaged. It will be our little secret. When you go off to Louisiana or Texas or Mexico or the western frontier, you will know that I will be wearing this ring."

Lyss was in no rush to confront the Colonel. Neither was he anxious to write a letter to his father telling that he intended to marry a planter's daughter.

"Our little secret," he replied.

"I will wait for you," she promised.

Cover Art: detail from reproduction -
        - original painting by Victor Anderson, circa 1928